# "I will fly out at the beginning of next week," she told him.

"Tell me when and I will arrange a plane. In fact," he added on a low note of delight, "I will fly you to Mardivino myself."

"'Oh, no, you won't, Nico," she said softly. "Once was enough!"

"You are criticizing my flying ability?"

"No, I am resisting your efforts to control me. You want my expertise and you'll get it, but you will be treated in exactly the same way as any other client. There will be no preferential treatment—not for you, and certainly not for me. I will take a scheduled airline flight, thank you very much, and I will add the cost to my bill."

For a moment he was speechless, scarcely able to believe what he was hearing. She was refusing his offer! To be flown to Mardivino by the youngest Prince of that principality!

**Harlequin Presents®**

Introduces a brand-new trilogy by
SHARON KENDRICK

THE
*ROYAL HOUSE*
OF
*CACCIATORE*

Passion, power & privilege—the dynasty
continues with these three handsome Princes…

Welcome to Mardivino—a beautiful and wealthy
Mediterranean island principality, with a
prestigious and glamorous royal family.
There are three Cacciatore princes—
Nicolo, Guido, and the eldest, the heir, Gianferro.

This month, meet Nico in
*The Mediterranean Prince's Passion*

In June, it's Guido's story:
*The Prince's Love-Child*
#2472

In July, it's Gianferro's turn:
*The Future King's Bride*
#2478

# Sharon Kendrick

## THE MEDITERRANEAN PRINCE'S PASSION

THE
ROYAL HOUSE
OF
CACCIATORE

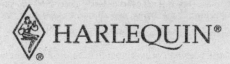

HARLEQUIN®

TORONTO • NEW YORK • LONDON
AMSTERDAM • PARIS • SYDNEY • HAMBURG
STOCKHOLM • ATHENS • TOKYO • MILAN • MADRID
PRAGUE • WARSAW • BUDAPEST • AUCKLAND

To the world's greatest historian,
the man whose name is synonymous with Gladstone
and fine wines, the erudite Professor Richard Shannon!

ISBN 0-373-12466-X

THE MEDITERRANEAN PRINCE'S PASSION

First North American Publication 2005.

Copyright © 2004 by Sharon Kendrick.

# CHAPTER ONE

IT WAS just a dazzle of white set against the endless sapphire, but the sun was blinding her too much to see clearly. Ella's eyes fluttered to a close in protest. Maybe she had imagined it. Like a person hallucinating an oasis in the desert, perhaps her mind had conjured up an image on the empty sea that surrounded them. Some sign of life other than the birds that circled and cawed in a sky as blue as the waters beneath.

'Mark.' She croaked the unfamiliar name through lips so parched they felt as if they had never tasted liquid before. 'Mark, are you there?' She racked her brains for one of the women's names. 'Helen!'

But there was no answer, and maybe that wasn't so surprising, for the throb, throb, throb of loud music from the lower deck drowned the sound of her feeble words. She could hear the muffled sound of girlish, drunken giggling drifting upwards. She moaned.

How long? How long since she had drunk anything? She knew she ought to go and get some water, but her legs felt as though they had been filled with lead. She lifted a heavy hand to try to brush the weight of damp hair that flopped so annoyingly against her cheek, but it fell uselessly to her side.

She was going to die. She knew she was.

She could feel the strength slowly ebbing from her body. Her ears were roaring and the weak flutter of her heart beat rapidly against her breast. Her skin was on fire, it was burning…burning…burning…

Below, the cool, darkened interior of the cabin beckoned to her enticingly, but an instinct even stronger than her need to escape the sun stopped her from giving in to it. Down there lay chaos, and no chance for escape, but at least here on deck someone might see her.

Her eyes began to close.

Please, God, let someone see her…

His dark hair ruffled by the breeze and his strong body relaxed, Nico stared at the horizon, his eyes suddenly narrowing as the flash of something on the horizon caught his attention.

A boat? Where there should be no boat? Here in the protected waters on this side of Mardivino? His mouth tightened. Modern-day bandits? Seeking access to the tax haven guarded so jealously by the super-rich? The island had a long history of being besieged by bounty-hunters and their modern-day counterparts—the paparazzi—and his face darkened. Where the hell were the Marine Patrol when you needed them?

But the devil-may-care facet of his character made his pulse begin to race with excitement. Ignoring—almost relishing—the potential danger to himself, he reached for the throttle and his jet-ski sped forward, roaring in a spray of foam towards the stricken craft, which bobbed like a child's toy on the waves.

As his craft approached he could see a figure lying on the deck, and as he drew alongside he could see that it was a woman and that she appeared to be sunbathing. Tawny limbs and tawny hair. Slim and supple, with the tight lushness of youth. It took him precisely two seconds to assess whether or not this was a ploy and she the decoy. It was an age-old method he had encountered before; it came with the territory he inhabited.

But she was not sunbathing. Something was very wrong—Nico could see that from her slumped and unmoving pose.

Moving swiftly, he secured his jet-ski and jumped on board, his stance alert and watchful as he scanned the deck for a brief moment and listened intently. From a distance he could hear the loud beat of dance music, but the woman appeared to be alone on deck.

In a few strides he had reached her. Bending over, he turned her onto her side, blotting out his instinctive first reaction to the way her magnificent breasts rose and fell beneath the skimpy jade-green bikini top she wore.

She was sick.

Assessingly, he ran his eyes over her. Her breathing was shallow, her eyes tight-closed and her skin very pink. He laid a brief exploratory hand on her forehead and felt the heat sizzling from it. Fever. Probably sunstroke, by the look of her.

Urgently, he shook her. *'Svegli!'* he ordered, but there was no response. He tried in French. *'Reveillez-vous!'* And then, louder, in Spanish. *'Despierte!'*

Through the mists of the dream that was sucking her down towards a black numbness Ella heard a deep voice urging her back to the surface, back towards the light. But the light was hurting her eyes and she didn't want to go there. She shook her head from side to side.

*'Wake up!'*

Her eyes flickered open. A face was looming over her—its hard, handsome features set in a look of grim concern. A dark angel. She *must* be dreaming. Or dying.

'Oh, no!' he exclaimed, and levered her up into his arms, supporting her head with an unmoving hand as it threatened to flop back. 'You will not sleep again! Do you hear me? Wake up! Wake up now, this instant. I demand it!'

The richly accented voice was too commanding to ignore, but Ella was lost in the grip of a fever too powerful to resist.

'Go away,' she mumbled, and she felt a cold terror when he lowered her back onto the deck and did just that—left her all alone again. She gave a little whimper.

Nico went below deck and the noise hit him like a

wall. He stood for a moment, studying the scene of decadence that lay before him.

He could count five people—three men and two women—and all of them were in advanced stages of intoxication. One woman was topless and snoring quietly on the floor, while another gyrated in front of one of the men like a very poor lap-dancer.

Only one of the men seemed to notice his arrival, and he raised a half-empty bottle of Scotch.

'Hey! Who're you?' he slurred.

Nico gave him a look of simmering fury. 'Are you aware that you're trespassing?' he snapped.

'No, matey—I think *you're* the one doing that! This boat I paid through the nose for, and—' The man pointed exaggeratedly upwards. 'The sea is free!' he added, in a sing-song voice.

'Not here, it isn't. You're in forbidden waters.' And, turning on his heel, Nico went back up onto the deck. He slid a mobile phone from his back pocket and punched in a number known to only a very few, which connected him straight to the Chief of Police.

'*Pronto? Si. Nicolo.*' He spoke rapidly in Italian.

There was a pause.

'You want that we should arrest them, Principe?' asked the Capo quietly.

Nico gave a hard glimmer of a smile. '*Si.* Why not? A night in jail sobering up might teach them never to put themselves nor others in danger again.' But he stared down thoughtfully at the girl, for she was not drunk; she was sick.

He bent down and shook her gently by the shoulder. Her eyes fluttered open, dazed and green as spring grass.

Through the haze of her fever she saw his strength—a rock, a safe harbour and her only means of escape. 'Don't leave me,' she begged.

The raw emotion in her voice made him still momentarily but it was an unnecessary appeal for he had already made up his mind. 'I have no intention of leaving you,' he said tersely, and scooped her up into his arms before she could protest.

Her arms clasped tightly around his neck, she slumped against his chest like a rag doll in an unconscious attitude of complete trust. He gripped her tightly as he manoeuvred her onto the jet-ski.

Most men would have struggled to cope with a woozy female, but Nico had been born to respond to challenge—it was one of the few things in life that invigorated him. A small smile touched the corners of his mouth as he set off for the shore.

He was always trying new thrills and spills, but this was the first time he'd ever rescued a damsel in distress.

## CHAPTER TWO

COOL dampness rippled enchanting fingers across her cheeks and Ella let out a small sigh.

'Mmm! S'nice!'

'Drink this!'

It was the voice that wouldn't go away. The voice that wouldn't take no for an answer. The voice that had been popping in and out of her consciousness with annoying frequency. A bossy, foreign voice, but an irresistible one, too.

Obediently Ella opened her lips and sipped again from the cup she was being offered, only this time she drank more greedily than before, gulping it so that the water ran in riveluts down her face, trickling over her chin and startling her out of the hazy fog that engulfed her.

'That is better,' said the deep voice, with a touch of approval. 'Take some more still, and then open your eyes properly.'

Befuddled, she did as she was told—only to find herself even more confused. For there was a man standing over her—a man she didn't recognise.

Or did she?

She blinked up at his face and something peculiar

happened to her already unsteady heart-rate, for he was utterly spectacular.

His chiselled features gave his face a hard, autocratic appearance, but a sensual mouth softened it. Narrowed eyes were fringed by blocks of dark lashes and his hair was jet-dark and wavy, and slightly too long. He looked rugged and powerful—familiar and yet a stranger. His skin was golden and olive and glowing—as though it had been gently lit from within. His was the face that had drifted in and out of her fevered sleep, coaxing and cooling her. A dark angel. A guardian angel.

So she had not been dreaming at all. Nor, it seemed, had she died.

Still blinking in consternation, she glanced around her. She was in a room—a very plain and simple room, containing little more than a small wooden table and a couple of old chairs. On the floor were worn floorboards, the walls were wooden, too, and she could hear the roar of waves. It was cool and dim and she was lying on a low kind of bed, beneath a tickly-feeling thing that was too thick to be a sheet and too thin to be a blanket. Her hand slithered inside.

*She was wearing nothing but a man's T-shirt!*

The last of her lethargy fled in an instant and fear galloped in to take its place. Clutching the coverlet, she sat up and stared at the man who stood over her, his dark face shuttered and watchful. Was she certain that she wasn't dreaming? Who was he, and what was she doing here?

'Would you mind telling me what the hell's going on?' she demanded breathlessly.

'I think…' There was a pause. He watched her very carefully, like a hunter with his prey held firmly in his sights. 'That I should be asking you that very same question.'

Her heart was pounding like a piston. His voice was soft and rich and accented. And accusing. When surely, if there was any accusing to be done… Beneath the coverlet she ran an exploratory hand down over her body, as if checking that all her limbs were intact. And not just her limbs…

Nico watched her. 'Oh, do not worry,' he drawled. 'Your virtue is intact. Or at least as intact as it was when you arrived.' Though God only knew what she had been up to with the band of drunks on board that boat.

Ella tried to will her stubborn memory into gear, but it was as if her brain had been wrapped in cotton wool. Something told her that she must be grateful to this man, but something about his dark masculinity was suddenly making her feel very shy. More than shy. 'What's happened?'

'You have been sick,' he explained, but his eyes lost nothing of their glittering suspicion.

She looked around for signs that she might be in a hospital, but there was nothing remotely medical or sterile about the place. In fact, there were grains of sand on the floorboards, and a wetsuit lay coiled in a heap like a seal skin. Some of the cotton wool cleared. 'Where am I?'

'Ah! At last! The traditional question. It took you long enough to ask,' he observed, arching imperious eyebrows that shot up into the ebony tumble of his hair. His dark eyes fixed her with a lancing stare.

'I'm asking now.'

The eyes narrowed, for he was unused to such a response. 'You don't know?'

'Why would I bother asking you if I already knew?'

Unless, he pondered, she had her own separate agenda, and there was no way of finding out, not until she was properly recovered. Not when she was still…

Nico turned away from her body, its outline undisguised by the T-shirt, its firm curves spelling out a temptation that would have stretched the resolve of the most holy and celibate of men—two things of which he had never been accused.

For hours she had lain there, her tawny limbs and hair flailing as she thrashed and cried out, hot with fever and lost in the strange world of delirium. And he had bathed her. Sponged her down. Fed her with water and sat with her during the long, lonely hours till dawn.

It had been a new sensation for him—having someone reliant and dependent on *him*. She had been as helpless as a wounded animal, and that very help-lessness had brought about a protectiveness he had never before experienced.

Until…

He had been smoothing the damp hair away from her sweat-sheened skin, murmuring words of comfort, when she had suddenly called out in alarm. And when he shushed her she had sat up, the sheet falling from her. The T-shirt he had hastily flung on her had man-aged to both conceal and reveal—and the hazy hint of glorious rose-tipped breast beneath had been en-chanting beyond belief. He had tried to move away but she had lifted her arms and clung onto him with the terrified and irresistible strength of someone who was lost in a nightmare. And she had been close. Oh…so…close… Far too close for comfort and sane thought.

His body had sprung into instant and unwilling re-sponse as she'd pressed closer still. Nerves stretching with unbearable tension, he had stared down into her eyes—the most green and startling eyes he had ever seen—but they had been clouded and vacant. Whomever or whatever she was seeing, it certainly was not him.

'Lie down on the bed!' he had ordered harshly, in English, and the still-dry lips had puckered into the shape of a parched flower before much-needed rain fell onto it.

Some men would have thought—why not? *Taja*

*ch'e e rosso*, as the Romans sometimes said. To have taken advantage of what was so beautifully on offer might have been an option, but Nico was of different blood from other men. Even if his hadn't been an appetite jaded by what had always been given to him so freely, he could not have countenanced making love to a woman unless she was in total command of her senses.

He stared down at her now and saw that the wild, febrile light had left her eyes. He felt a small tug of triumph, for she had been in his charge and now she was recovered. 'Are you hungry?' he asked unexpectedly.

His words made Ella focus, not on the extraordinary situation in which she found herself, but on the needs of her body, and she suddenly realised that her stomach felt empty and her head light as air. Hungry? She was absolutely starving!

'Why, yes,' she said, in surprise.

'Then you must eat.' He began to move away, as if he couldn't wait to put physical distance between them.

'No—wait!'

He stilled at her words, a bemused expression on his lean and handsome face. How long had it been since someone had issued such a curt order? 'What is it?'

'How long have I been here?' she questioned faintly.

'Only a day.'

Only a day? *Only a day!* She shook her head again to clear it, and strands of memory began to filter back. A boat. A boat trip taken with a bunch of people who, it had turned out, knew nothing of basic maritime law or safety. Who had proceeded to drink themselves into oblivion. And a man who had invited her—who had clearly thought that a woman should pay the traditional price for a luxury weekend.

She screwed up her nose. What had his name been?

Mark! Yes, that was it. Mark.

Her eyes now accustomed to the dim light within the interior of the room, Ella turned her head slowly to look around.

'Where's Mark? What's happened to him?'

Nico's mouth hardened. Had 'Mark' been on her mind when she had pressed her body so close to his? Or was she the kind of woman who was naturally free with her body?

'By now—' he glanced at his watch '—he will just about be released from jail.'

'Jail!' She stared at him in confusion. 'How come?'

'Because I informed the local police of their trespass,' he informed her coolly.

'You've had him put in *jail*?'

'Not him,' he corrected. 'Them. All of them.'

Ella swallowed, suddenly fearful. Just where *was* she? And who the hell was *he*? 'Isn't that a bit over the top?'

'You think so?' His voice became filled with contempt. 'Putting the trespass aside—you think it acceptable for people to be drunk in charge of a powerful boat? To put not only their own lives in danger, but those of others? And that includes you! What do you think might have happened if I hadn't come along?'

Something in the stark accusation of his words made her feel very small and very vulnerable. 'L-look, I'm very grateful for everything you've done,' she said, in a low trembling voice, 'but would you mind telling me exactly what's going on? I don't—'

He silenced her with an autocratic wave of his hand. 'No more questions. Not now. Later you will ask me whatever you please and I shall answer it, but first you must eat. You have been sick. You are weak and you are hungry and you need food. You will have your answers, but later.'

Ella opened her mouth to object, and then shut it again, realising that she was in no position to do so. And even if she had been she simply did not have the strength. He was right—she felt all weak and woolly with the aftermath of fever.

Yet surely she wasn't expected to just lie here, helpless beneath the cover, while this handsome, dominant stranger told her what she could and couldn't do? But what was the alternative? Did she just leap out of bed, feeling strangely naked despite his T-shirt?

He turned his head to look at her and saw the fleeting look of vulnerability that had melted away her objections. Only this time he had to force himself to respond to it. Before it had been easy. While she had been sick he had been able to be gentle with her, as he would have with a child. But now that she was awake it was different. And suddenly not so easy. For she was a beautiful, breathing woman and not a child.

Almost without thinking Nico rebuilt the familiar emotional barriers with which he habitually surrounded himself.

'You wish to wash, perhaps?'

'Please.' But she noticed that his voice had grown cool.

He pointed to a curtain at the far end of the simple room. 'You'll find some basic facilities through there,' he said. He pulled a fresh T-shirt down from an open shelf and threw it onto the divan.

'You might want that,' he said. 'All your stuff is still on the boat and your bikini is hanging outside. I washed it,' he explained, amused to see her look of barely concealed horror. Was she afraid he was expecting her to change in front of him? Then clearly she had no memory of how her T-shirt had slithered up her naked thighs as she had thrashed around. Of how *he* had played the gentleman and slithered it right down again. 'Don't be shy—I'll be outside.'

*Don't be shy!* Ella watched him disappearing through the door, caught a dazzling glimpse of blue as it opened, and heard the hypnotic pounding music of the waves.

She was obviously in some kind of beach hut—but *where* exactly?

She stared at the closed door and half thought of running after him, and demanding some answers. But she was too weak to run anywhere, and she was also naked, sticky and dusty. Surely she would be better placed to ask for explanations once she was dressed?

Never had the thought of washing seemed more alluring, though the sight that greeted her behind the curtain was not terribly reassuring. There was a sink, a loo, and the most ancient-looking shower that Ella had ever seen. It didn't gush, it trickled, but at least it was halfway warm and there was soap and shampoo, too—surprisingly luxurious brands for such a spartan setting.

Basic it might have been, but Ella had never enjoyed or appreciated a shower more than that one. She washed all the salt and sand away from her skin and hair, and roughly towelled herself dry, then slithered into the clean T-shirt that fortunately—because its owner was so tall—came to mid-way down her thigh. It wasn't what she would call decent, but it was better than nothing.

He was standing by the small table, dishing out two plates of something she didn't recognise, the scent of which made her empty stomach ache. He had left the door open and Ella discovered why the sound of the waves was so loud. It looked directly out onto the most glorious sea view she had ever seen in her life.

Pale, powdered sand dotted with shells gave way to white-topped sapphire waves that glittered and sparkled and danced and filled the room with light. But the room seemed suddenly to have kaleidoscoped in on itself, for all Ella could see was the dark power of the man who was silhouetted against the brilliant backdrop outside.

Now that she was on her feet she didn't need the T-shirt as an indicator of just how tall he was. She could see that instantly from the way he towered, dominating the small room, making everything else shrink into insignificance. His hair was dark and ruffled, tiny tendrils of it curling onto the back of his neck. She felt an odd, powerful kick to her heart as he looked up and slowly drifted his eyes over her.

'My T-shirt suits you,' he mused softly.

It was an innocent enough remark, but something in the way he said it, and the accompanying look of approbation in his eyes, made her feel all woman. She could feel her breasts tingling, and the soft, moist ache of longing. It was a powerful and primitive response, and it had never happened to her quite like that before.

Filled with a sudden feeling of claustrophobia, and unsure of how to deal with the situation, she walked to the open door and breathed in the fresh, salty tang of the air, staring at the moving water in silence for a moment.

'Beautiful, isn't it?' came his voice from behind her.

Composing her face into an expression of innocent appreciation, Ella turned round. 'Unbelievable.' And so was he. Oh, he was just gorgeous. 'That…that smells good,' she managed, in an effort to distract herself.

'Mmm.' He had seen the perking breasts and the brief darkening of her eyes and he felt himself harden. 'Come and eat,' he said evenly. 'We could take our food outside, but I think you need a break from the sun. So we'll just look at the view from here.'

But Ella didn't move. 'You said you would give me some answers, and I'd like some. Now. Please.'

Nico gave a slow smile. The novel always stirred his blood, and it was rare for him to be spoken to with anything other than deference. 'Questions can wait, *cara*, but your hunger cannot.'

His words were soft, but a steely purposefulness underpinned them. As if he were used to issuing orders; as if he would not tolerate those orders being disobeyed. The scent of the food wafted towards her and Ella felt her mouth begin to water. Maybe he was right. Again.

She went back inside and sat down at the table.

'Eat,' he said, pushing a plate of food towards her, but it seemed the command was unnecessary. She had begun to devour the dish, falling on it with the fervour of the truly hungry.

He watched her in fascinated silence, for this, too, was a new sensation. In his company people always picked uninterestedly at their food. There were unspoken rules that were always followed. They waited for him to begin and they finished when he finished. It was all part of the protocol that surrounded him—and yet for all the notice she took of him he might as well not have been there!

She ate without speaking, unable to remember ever having enjoyed a meal as much. Eventually she put her fork down and sighed.

'It's good?'

'It's delicious.'

'Hunger makes the best sauce,' he observed slowly.

There was red wine in front of her, and he gestured towards it, but she shook her head and drank some water instead, then sat back in her chair and fixed him with a steady look. His eyes were as black as a moonless night and they lanced through her with their ebony light.

'Now are you going to start explaining?'

Nico found that he was enjoying himself. He had played the rescuer—so let him have a little amusement in return. 'Tell me what you wish to know.'

'Well, for a start—who are you? I don't even know your name, Mr...?'

There was a pause while he considered the question. It seemed sincere enough, although the Mr tacked onto the end could have been disingenuous, of course. Was it?

'It is Nico,' he said eventually. From behind the thick dark lashes that shielded his eyes he watched her reaction carefully, but there was no sign of recognition in her emerald eyes. 'And you?'

'I'm Ella.'

Ella. Yes. 'It's a pretty name.'

'It's short for Gabriella.'

'Like the angel,' he murmured, letting his eyes drift carelessly over the pale flames of her hair.

It was that thing in his voice again—that murmured caress that made her conscious of herself as a woman. And him as a man. A man who had seen her sick and half-naked. But he was the angel—a guardian angel.

'Where am I?' she asked slowly.

Now his expression became sceptical. 'You really don't know?'

She sighed. 'How long are we going to continue with these guessing games? Of course I don't know. One minute I was on a boat—and the next I'm in some kind of beach hut, eating...' She stared down at her empty plate. Even the food had been unfamiliar, just as he was, with his strange accent and his exotic looks. Disorientated, she found herself asking, 'What have I just eaten?'

'Rabbit.'

'Rabbit,' she repeated dully. She had never eaten rabbit in her life!

'They run wild in the hillsides,' he elaborated, and then, still watching her very closely, he said, 'Of Mardivino.'

'Mardivino?' She stared at him as it began to sink in. 'Is that where we are?'

'Indeed it is.' He sipped from a tumbler of dark wine and surveyed her from eyes equally dark. 'You have heard of it?'

It was one of the less-famous principalities. A sun-drenched Mediterranean island—tax haven and home to many of the world's millionaires. Exclusive and remote and very, very beautiful.

'I'm not a complete slouch at geography,' she said. 'Of course I've heard of it.'

Authority reasserted itself. 'You were in forbidden waters. You should never have ventured onto this side of the island!'

She remembered Mark and one of the others blustering about navigation, and then they had started hitting the bottle, big-time. She remembered how frightened she had been, how she had stood on deck for what seemed like hours and hours, the blistering sun beating down on her quite mercilessly. She shivered. 'But we were lost,' she protested. 'Genuinely lost!'

'Yes.' He didn't disbelieve her. Off Mardivino's rugged northern coast there were rocks and rip tides that would challenge all but the most experienced sailor. No one would have been foolish enough to deliberately put themselves in the danger in which he had found them. So why had they?

His eyes bored into her. 'Those people with you...'

'What about them?'

There was a long pause. 'One of them is a journalist, perhaps?' he questioned casually.

'A journalist?' She screwed up her nose. 'Well, I don't know any of them that well, but none of them said they were journalists.' She met his eyes, which were hard and glittering with suspicion. 'Why would they be?'

'No reason,' he said swiftly.

But Ella heard the evasion in his voice and stared at him. Nothing added up. She stared at him as if seeing him properly for the first time. His clothes were simple, but his bearing was aristocratic, and there was something about his appearance that she had never seen in a man before. Something in the way he carried himself—an arrogant kind of self-assurance that seemed innate rather than learned. Yet he wore faded jeans and a worn T-shirt...

He had brought her to this beach hut, where the shower dripped in a single trickle and yet the soap and shampoo were the finest French brands. She frowned. And he had called her *cara*, hadn't he?

'Are you Italian?'

He shook his head.

'Spanish?'

'No.'

'French, then?'

He smiled. 'Still no.'

Words he had spoken came back to her. 'Yet you speak all three languages?'

He shrugged. How much to tell her? How long to continue this delicious game of anonymity? How long *could* he? 'Indeed I do.'

'And your English is perfect.'

'I know it is,' he agreed mockingly.

This time she would not be deterred by the soft, seductive voice. Ella leaned across the table, challenging him with her eyes. 'Just who exactly *are* you, Nico?'

# CHAPTER THREE

THE strangest thing was that Nico was really enjoying himself. It was like a game, or a story—the one where a prince disguised himself as a beggar and no one recognised him.

For a man whose life had been composed of both light and dark fairy tale aspects, it was a new and entertaining twist. And if he told her…then what? Nothing would be the same, not ever again. Her attitude towards him would change irrevocably. No longer would she speak to him as if were just a man—an ordinary man.

When he was a little boy, had he not sometimes wished to be made 'normal', just for the day? And even when he had been at college in America, doing his best to blend in, people had still known of his identity. It had been inevitable—security had arrived before he had, to make the place fit for a prince.

And since when had he been asked to make an account of himself? To explain who he was and his place in the world?

Never.

He leaned back in the wooden chair. 'How does a man define himself?' He asked the question as much of himself as of her. 'Through his possessions? His achievements, perhaps?'

Ella gave him a bemused look. 'Are you incapable of giving a direct answer to a direct question?'

Probably. In the world he inhabited he was never asked a direct question. Conversation was left for him to lead, at whim. It was forbidden by ancient decrees for others to initiate it. When he spoke people listened. He had never known anything else, had accepted it as the norm, but now—with a tug of unfamiliar awareness—he recognised that total deference could be limiting.

'I am Nico,' he said slowly. 'You know my name. I'm twenty-eight and I was born on Mardivino—a true native of the principality.' His eyes glittered. 'So now you know everything.'

'Everything and yet nothing,' she challenged. 'What do you do?'

'Do?' His eyes glittered. How could he have forgotten that in her world people were defined by what they did for a living?

'For a living?'

'Oh, this and that,' he said evasively. 'I work for a very rich man.'

That might go some of the way towards explaining things. Maybe that was why he seemed so impressively self-assured. Perhaps he had picked up and now mirrored some of his rich employer's characteristics, as sometimes happened. That might also explain the extravagant soaps in the bathroom—he might be the recipient of a rich man's generosity.

Ella gestured towards the humble interior. 'And is this your home?'

There was a pause. 'No. No, I don't live here. It's just a place that belongs to my...employer.'

'And the jet-ski?'

'You remember that?' he questioned.

The food and the shower had worked a recuperative kind of magic, and more fragments of memory now began to filter back. She recalled being clasped against a firm, hard body and the comforting, safe warmth of him. Then fast bobbing across the water, with spray being thrown against her fevered skin.

'Kind of.'

'What about it?' he asked carelessly.

'Is it yours?'

Inexplicably, he felt a flicker of disappointment. Would that matter, then? A top-of-the-range jet-ski was a rich man's toy. His habitual cynicism kicked in. Of course it would matter—things like that always did. You were never seen for who you were but what you owned and what you possessed. Take away the trappings and what was left?

'No,' he said flatly. 'It's just something I use when I want to.'

'Well, I hope I'm not going to get you into trouble,' she ventured.

His cynical thoughts began to crumble when she looked at him like that. So...so *sweet*, he thought. So scrubbed and so innocent. So utterly relaxed in his company and now worrying about his welfare! And when had anyone ever done *that* before?

Now that it was dry, the tawny hair was spilling in profusion over her shoulders and face, but not quite managing to disguise the lush swell of her breasts. The aching in his body intensified as he imagined himself running the tips of his fingers over their heavy curves. 'No, you won't get me into trouble,' he murmured. 'I suspect he wouldn't have minded rescuing you himself.'

The words were flirty, and almost imperceptibly something in the atmosphere changed and then intensified. A blurry sexual awareness that had been there all the time was now brought into sharp focus. Ella felt the warm tongue of desire licking its way over her skin and the heated clamour of her response. She found that she didn't dare look at him—and yet where else was there to look? The room was so small, and he was so...so...

She swallowed, her mouth as dry as the sun-baked sand outside. 'Maybe I should think about getting home,' she said quietly.

Nico had watched her body tense, and then seen the wary look that crept into her eyes. He forced himself to steel against the demands of his hungry body, aware that he could frighten her away. Because sex was easy. He could get sex any time he wanted. But not a unique situation like this. And what would sex be like with a woman who *didn't know*?

'Not yet.' His dark eyes on her face, he took a mouthful of wine. 'You still haven't told me anything about you.'

'Well, you know my name. And I'm twenty-six and I was born in Somerset.' Her eyes mocked him. 'So now you know everything about me, too.'

'Everything and nothing.' He echoed her sardonic words. 'And what of the men on board—one of them is your lover, perhaps?'

Ella found her cheeks colouring. 'You can't just come out and ask me something like that!' she protested.

'Why not?'

'Because I thought we were sitting here having a polite conversation, and that sort of question breaks all the rules!'

'A polite conversation?' he murmured. 'Oh, I think not, *cara mia*. When a man and a woman talk together there is always an internal dialogue taking place. What you say is never what you're really thinking, deep down.' *Or else I would be telling you that I want to feel your naked body against me, to taste your tongue as it licks against my lips and hear your cry of startled pleasure as I thrust into you that sweet first•time.*

His murmured words increased her wariness, but heightened the sensation of tense expectation, too. Surely by now she should be itching to get away? Not finding her eyes drawn to the luscious curve of his lips, to the hard, clean lines of his body, and thinking how magnificent he must look when he was naked.

His voice interrupted her thoughts. 'So?' he persisted silkily. 'You wish to rush away to the jail-house to greet one of them?'

'Ugh—no, thanks!' Ella shuddered. 'None of them is my lover, nor ever would be. Mark is just someone I met through work.' She bit her lip, remembering how trusting she had been. 'He invited me along to join some friends of his for the weekend, only I arrived to discover that his idea about how we were going to spend our time together differed somewhat from mine.'

'So what happened?'

'I made it clear I wasn't interested in him, and that's when he decided to make love to a bottle of whisky instead.' She pulled a face. 'They all did.'

'And did he hurt you?' he demanded, his expression darkening.

Ella shook her head, taken aback by the sudden hardening of his voice. 'No. I stayed as far away from them as possible. Then they started to drink more and more, and no one seemed capable of taking charge of the boat.' Her voice trembled a little. 'That's when I started to get frightened.'

He remembered the way she had clung to him on deck, and the gut-wrenching effect of the little whimper of protest she had made when he had left her. The way she had weakly gripped onto his hand as if he were her lifeline. Playing rescuer to a woman could evoke some very powerful and primitive feelings, he recognised—feelings he was unfamiliar with, which were given extra potency by her ignorance of who he really was. And that, too, was a rare sensation.

He knew he wanted to make love to her, but he couldn't do it now. Not here. Making love to a woman on his own territory was always fraught with difficulty. And he had no wish to shatter her trust in him, nor to abuse his position. When he took her to bed it must be on equal terms. And in order for that to happen he must get her back to England with as little fuss as possible.

'You want to go home?' he asked suddenly.

His question took Ella off-guard, and she hoped her expression managed to mask her disappointment. What had she been expecting? To stay here indefinitely, in this beautiful place, with this strong, handsome man who had saved her? Alone like Adam and Eve—with the inevitable outcome of sexual discovery?

She fixed her mouth into a wobbly kind of smile. 'Well, I suppose I'd better.'

He heard her reluctance, and that only heightened his appetite. But, as he had already told her, hunger made the best sauce...

He slid a high tech-looking mobile phone from the back pocket of his jeans. 'I'll arrange it.'

He went outside to get a signal and she could hear him talking in a low, rapid voice in Spanish. Then he came back inside.

'We can be airborne within the hour.'

She was unable to hide her bewilderment. 'That soon? But my ticket is from Nice, and that's miles away.'

'We'll be travelling by private jet.'

Her frown deepened. 'How come?'

Again, his eyes pierced her with their brilliant light, but he was enjoying this sensation of anonymity far too much to break it. And besides, he wasn't telling a lie. He was merely presenting the truth in a slightly different form.

'My…employer,' he elaborated casually, 'is an exceedingly rich and generous man. And I'm a qualified pilot,' he added. 'So I can fly you home.' There was a pause and his dark eyes captured hers in their ebony crossfire. 'That is, of course, if you trust me to fly you home safely, *cara*?'

He had rescued her from the boat and ensured that she did not spend a night in the cells. He had cared for her while she thrashed around with fever—what was there *not* to trust?

And when he called her *cara* like that…

'But can you just get up and go like that? Won't your employer mind?'

'Not at all. I have to do some business myself in England, and I can do it this week just as easily as next.'

She saw the gleam of anticipation that had lightened the night-dark eyes, the slow smile that had irresistibly curved his lips, and she could feel the erratic beat of her heart.

'It's very…sweet of you,' she said.

The question *why* hung unspoken on the air.

He shook his head very slightly. It was a very English description, and one that had never been applied to him in his life. 'Sweet? No, *cara*—it is something much more fundamental than that.' He suddenly became aware of the irony of his words. 'You see, I find that I'm just as susceptible to the lure of a pair of dazzling green eyes and a pair of petal-soft lips as the next man.'

Ella felt the heat rise in her cheeks. It was most definitely an overture. And what was she going to do about it? After all, what did she have in common with this all-action foreigner—with his jet-ski and his pilot's licence and his ability to rustle up a delicious one-pot meal in the most basic surroundings? Who lived on a remote island far away from her world…

A shadow of a smile had flitted across the hard contours of his face. 'Maybe you'd like to have dinner with me back in England?' Breakfast would have been his meal of choice, but that would inevitably follow.

From the crashing of her heart against her ribcage someone might think that she'd never been asked out for dinner before—but quite honestly that was the way it felt. As though every invitation up until that moment had been a rehearsal for the real thing. And

Ella found herself smiling at him with lips that she had never considered to be petal-soft before, but that now parted like a flower.

'Why, thank you,' she murmured. 'I'd like that.'

# CHAPTER FOUR

IT'S ONLY a dinner date, Ella told herself.

So why did she feel so jumpy? Why were the hands that smoothed the dress down over her hips so clammy and her lips so cool and pale? She rubbed a slick of lipgloss on them and stared at herself critically in the mirror.

The silky black dress gleamed against the curve of bottom and breast, contrasting provocatively with the tiny covered buttons that ran in a demure line from neck to knee.

The spiky black sandals made the best of her legs, and her only adornment was a matching velvet choker at her neck, inlaid with jet as dark and glittering as Nico's eyes.

For the umpteenth time she glanced at the clock, nervously tugging at the hem of her dress, her mind skipping back over the extraordinary events of the last couple of days, which had culminated in Nico flying her home on a private jet.

Ella had spent the flight sipping on a fruit cocktail and looking around her with a sense of disbelief. Whatever Nico's boss did for a living, he must be enormously successful at it to own a plane like that.

She had glanced yet again to the cockpit, to see

Nico sitting in front of a radar screen lit up like a Christmas tree, his fingers caressing the joy stick as if it was a woman's body, and she had shivered, unable to prevent herself. There was something decidedly sexy about a man who could fly a plane—but there again, she'd never met one before!

'Here you are. Home,' Nico murmured as he came through into the cabin after a successful touch-down, his eyes shining.

When he flew a plane he always felt filled with a wild kind of exhilaration—it was the same when he sailed, or climbed, or dived deep to explore the beautiful coral reefs off Mardivino. Some people called it living dangerously—he just called it living.

'Thanks,' Ella said steadily, praying that he'd meant his offer of dinner. 'It was a brilliant flight.'

'So when am I going to see you?' he drawled. 'Tonight?'

It nearly killed her, but Ella shook her head. A woman should never be *too* available—everyone in the world knew *that*! 'No, not tonight, I'm afraid. I have masses to catch up on.'

He raised his eyebrows. 'Cancel it,' he said arrogantly.

Their eyes clashed. That was what he was used to, she recognised. Easy come, easy go. Well, if he wasn't prepared to wait even a day, then he was wasting his time.

'Sorry,' she said coolly. 'I can't. I've been away

and I need to catch up on work. See what's been happening in my absence. You know.'

With an effort he hid the little flicker of irritation and shrugged. 'Sure. So…when? Tomorrow night—or will you be busy then, too?'

She heard the sarcasm in his voice. 'Tomorrow will be fine,' she said steadily, but the small victory of holding out only increased her sense of apprehension.

She wasn't dealing with the kind of man she normally came into contact with—Nico was different, and not just because he was foreign and heart-stoppingly gorgeous. He flew planes and plucked women to safety from lost boats. He was, she recognised, a true alpha male, with the corresponding appetites, and she hadn't run into enough of them to be quite sure of how to deal with him…

'Give me your address,' he said. 'I'll come and pick you up around eight. We'll go somewhere local—unless you'd rather meet up in London?'

Ella's mind raced. London would throw up its own problems—like getting back late after dinner and him suggesting a hotel. And she had never been the kind of woman to fall into bed with a man on a first date. Slightly appalled at the progression of her thoughts, Ella shook her head. 'We have a lovely restaurant, close to where I live. I'll take you there.'

At just after eight Nico jammed his finger on the doorbell, the scent of flowers drifting in the warm, heavy air towards him. Summer roses flowered in profusion around the door of her cottage—which looked as pretty as a picture you might see on an old-fashioned box of chocolates.

He felt a sense of vague detachment, as if he couldn't quite believe where he was or what he was doing—a million miles away from his usual world and all its restraints and rules.

The door opened and suddenly he could barely think straight, for she looked utterly sensational, wearing a clinging black dress that made her body look as if it was coated in liquorice. And he could lick it all off...

A slow smile curved his mouth. '*Ciao*, Ella,' he said softly.

Ella stared at him and words just refused to come—because... Oh, he really *was* gorgeous.

On Mardivino she had been captivated by his powerful strength and his spell-bindingly good looks, but now those qualities were somehow increased a thousandfold. Maybe it was seeing him away from his natural habitat—like plucking an exotic flower and placing it in a suburban garden.

His height made the proportions of her rose-covered porch resemble a doll's house, and next to him even the softly brilliant colours of the garden flowers faded into insignificance. His skin gleamed faintly olive, and he was wearing soft, cool linen through which the hard, muscular power of his body was startlingly evident. His dark eyes gleamed with brilliance, and here, under a gentler English sun, he looked almost indecently alive—as though any other man in the world would look like only half a man next to him.

Her heart began to thunder erratically and her mouth dried to sawdust. 'Hello, Nico.'

It occurred to him that she might have been doing her homework on Mardivino and that things might already have irrevocably changed. Did she know? He stared at her closely but her eyes showed no indication that she found out. He raised his eyebrows in lazy question. 'Hungry?'

She felt as if food would choke her—but that was hardly the most diplomatic thing to say before a dinner date. 'I…I hope you like the restaurant,' she said breathlessly, for his warm, virile scent seemed to be running heated fingertips over her skin.

He smiled with satisfaction, enjoying her response. The unspoken question was already answered in his mind—for the wide-eyed look of pleasure that made her green eyes sparkle like emeralds convinced him that to her he was still just 'Nico'.

'You look very beautiful,' he said softly.

Oddly enough, his flattery had the reverse effect to the one she suspected he wanted. It brought her to her senses. Made her see things for what they really were, and not how she would like them to be. She was not beautiful—she was reasonably attractive on a good day.

'Mediterranean men are always better at giving

compliments than their English counterparts,' she observed coolly.

'Which might explain why Mediterranean women are more gracious at accepting them,' he countered wryly.

Oh, if only she could rewind the clock and play that scene again! Was she going to ruin the evening before it had even started? She gave him an apologetic smile. 'You're right.'

'Shall we try again?' he mocked, curving his lips into a smile. 'You look very beautiful.'

'Thank you.'

'You're welcome.'

Her heart pounded. When he looked at her like that she wished... She wished he would pull her into his arms and kiss her. She wanted to touch her fingertips to his cheek, as if to assure herself that he was flesh and blood and not some figment of her imagination. But she stopped herself.

'Would you...um, would you like a drink first?' she asked. 'Or shall we just get going?'

She was like a lioness protecting her den, thought Nico, and clearly nervous about letting him set foot over the threshold! He had never had to play by the rules of other men before, and now he was beginning to see the disadvantages.

He shook his dark head, recognising the need to get her on neutral territory. 'No. Let's go and eat,' he said.

It was too warm for her to need a coat or wrap,

and they walked side by side down the village street, which was washed amber with the light of the sun. An old man was in his front garden, dead-heading his roses, and he smiled at them as they passed.

'Beautiful evening, isn't it?'

'It's gorgeous,' said Ella, stealing a look at Nico's hard, dark profile.

The restaurant was nestled into a crook of the high street, right next to the church. It was small, and run by an enthusiastic amateur, but word had spread about its fresh, seasonal food, and in high season it was nearly always full and notoriously hard to get a booking. But on fine nights they put more tables out on the terrace and down onto the lawn beyond, and to-night was one of them.

Ella saw a couple of women turn their heads and stare hard at them as they wended their way to a table beneath a chestnut tree. Maybe she shouldn't be surprised—Nico *was* exceptionally good-looking, and he really *did* stand out in a crowd. And there weren't exactly many Latin hunks strolling round the streets of Greenhampton!

'You must order for me, *cara*,' he said firmly once they had sat down, handing his menu straight back to the waitress.

'What do you like?'

'Everything. I like everything.' His eyes were steady as they rested on her face. 'I have very catholic tastes.'

Oh, heavens... Ella was aware of a sudden wave

of helpless longing as she was caught in the soft ebony light from his eyes. It was as if a man had never looked at her before—though when she stopped to think about it no man had—not with such an undeniable message of sensuality. Yet his silent flirting did nothing to detract from his cool air of self-possession, which seemed so at odds with his warmly Latin exterior.

She ordered asparagus and prawns and chilled Montrachet, unable to miss the unmistakably flirtatious glance the waitress slanted at him—though to his credit he didn't react in any way.

The sky was a pale Wedgwood blue, softened with apricot edges from the sun. In the distance could be heard the sporadic sound of birdsong and the occasional rattling brush of crickets. Nico had deliberately sat with his back to the other diners, and now he drank a glass of wine and expelled a long, low sigh as he felt all the tension leave his body.

'That's good wine,' he murmured.

She looked up. 'I know it is.'

He laughed, and captured her eyes. 'So, have you lived here a long time?'

'About three years. I went to university nearby and liked it a lot—but it wasn't until I knew what I wanted to do that I put down roots.'

He ran the tips of his fingers reflectively around his chilled glass. 'I don't really know anything about you,' he observed.

'No.' Ella laughed. 'Maybe it's because of the peculiar way we met.'

Her phrase had the slight resonance of permanence about it, and made him slightly wary—until he reminded himself that women had a habit of making every new encounter sound as though it was a contender for the *Romeo and Juliet* stakes. And if he wanted her—which he did—then surely he should indulge her?

He sipped his wine. 'So tell me about yourself.'

'Well, I studied History at university.' She drew a deep breath, then told him about leap-frogging from job to job, about never quite feeling any real satisfaction in her work and being unable to settle to anything, until one day an American cousin of hers had complained that it was impossible to discover the 'real' England—that everywhere was just a plastic Ye Olde Teashoppe-type experience. Foreign visitors wanted to see places off the beaten track, places of historic interest and wonderful gardens that weren't completely overrun by day-trippers with cameras.

'So you saw a gap in the market?' he guessed.

'Absolutely. I sourced all the best small castles and country houses and found comfortable non-chain hotels. I went looking for simple restaurants—ones like this—the kind of places you wouldn't normally get to hear about. I took a loan from the bank, founded the Real England Tour Company, advertised on the Internet and the business has just taken off. I've even got someone working with me now.'

'Wow.' His eyes gleamed. 'I'm impressed.'

'So that's me.' Ella put her elbows on the table and, leaning forward, rested her chin in her hands. 'What about you?'

They both watched in silence while the waitress put their food down in front of them. They stared at it as if it was an unwelcome intruder.

Nico ate a prawn, more for convention than hunger's sake. 'Actually, I work in tourism myself—but in a different kind of way.'

'Really? Like what?'

'Well, it's complicated. It would take hours to explain.' And he didn't have hours. Not to spend on talking. He leaned towards her and the faint scent of lilac drifted to him. 'Let's not talk about boring stuff like jobs, Ella. Because on a night like this the stuff we aren't saying is deafening us—can't you hear it?'

She stared straight into his eyes, feeling herself beginning to melt, knowing what was coming next and both scared and longing to hear it. 'Stuff like...like what?'

'Like the fact that I have waited just as long as it is possible to wait and now I want to kiss you. And that if we order any more food it is going to be completely wasted because I would prefer to take you back home, where I can kiss you in private.' His dark eyes glittered unrepentantly as they lingered on her lips. 'Shocked?' he drawled.

'Not shocked, no,' she said slowly, because his

words had scraped sharp, jagged fingernails over her senses, leaving her raw and aching.

There had been men she had wanted before, of course there had, but never like this—with a wave of longing so powerful that it seemed to have punched out all her breath and heartbeat and sense and reason. She shook her head again.

'What, then, if not shocked?' he murmured.

His eyes caressed her and she could feel the warm, honeyed throb of her blood urging her on, compelling her to tell him what she really wanted.

'Impatient, I guess,' she said huskily, and swallowed.

His eyes narrowed, her reaction taking him momentarily by surprise—but the unexpected was a very potent aphrodisiac. He withdrew a wallet, peeled off several notes and threw them down on the table.

'This was supposed to be my treat for all your help,' Ella protested.

'Shut up,' he said softly.

'And you've left far too much,' she commented as he stood up.

'Then it will be a pleasant surprise for the waitress, won't it?'

She hoped he could afford it—that he wasn't making an expansive gesture just for the sake of impressing her. But then he was putting his arm around her shoulders, and his fingertips were brushing against her bare skin, and all she could think about was his touch.

They walked breathlessly into the street, and as

soon as they were out of sight of the customers he pulled her hard against him, choosing a darkened alcove where they could not be seen—like a college boy who wanted to get intimate without ruining his bachelor reputation.

It seemed to have taken a long time to get here, but at last she was in his arms, and he was kissing her, and she was kissing him back, and suddenly things began to spin out of control.

# CHAPTER FIVE

'Nico!' Ella gasped as his lips drove down on hers, shocking and cajoling them into an instant, yielding response.

'*Si? Che cosa?*' he whispered impatiently, circling his hips against her and hearing with triumph yet another gasp.

'We can't do this!' She closed her eyes as he blatantly pressed the rock-hard cradle of his desire against her. 'Not here!'

Nico stilled. She thought he was going to take her there? Unzip himself and pull her panties down and do it up against a wall? His desire rocketed almost out of control and he pulled his mouth away and closed his eyes, trying desperately to steady his breathing.

'Let's go,' he bit out.

He took her hand and Ella let him, in such a daze that it might as well have been *his* village, not hers, as she blindly mirrored his footsteps until they arrived back at the cottage.

Her hands were trembling so much as she tried to unlock the door that he took the key from her. Once they were inside the hall, he turned to her, lifted her chin and stared down into her troubled face, creasing his forehead into a frown. 'What is it?'

'What must you think of me?' she breathed.

Ah! He hid a smile. He knew this game. Women wanted sex just as much as men did, but nature made them need to dress it up as respectable—if sex could ever be described in such a way.

'What do I think? I think you are very beautiful, *cara*, and I want to make love to you very much.'

She pulled away from him, her eyes dark with hunger—but years of conditioning was hard to get rid of in just a couple of short hours. She pointed towards the kitchen. 'Maybe...maybe I should make us some coffee?'

For a moment he was incredulous. She had been in his arms, just seconds away from instant surrender, and now she was distancing herself? It was unknown—and unheard of! A pulse beat deep in his groin. If he moved towards her again and touched her would she have the strength to repeat her actions? He thought not.

But something stopped him, and it was more than the unimaginable idea that she might hold firm in her resolve. No, once again it was the tantalising prospect of experiencing what other men must encounter every day of their lives. Having to fight for what they wanted.

For once the playing field was equal, when usually all the odds were stacked high in his favour. Had he not wondered over the years what it would be like if a woman treated him as a normal man, knowing that it was unlikely ever to happen? Well, now he had the chance to find out for himself.

The gods had blessed him with looks and brains, as well as the honour and burden of his birthright—so let him see whether they alone were enough to achieve what he so achingly wanted.

'Maybe you should,' he agreed, his voice silky with consideration.

Ella bit her lip. Hadn't part of her been hoping—praying—that he would arrogantly override her doubts and fears by taking her in his arms and kissing them all away?

'Would…would you like some?' To her horror and her consternation she began to tremble violently, and Nico watched her from narrowed eyes before lifting his hand to trace a thoughtful finger around the edge of her lips. 'Do you know what I think?' he whispered.

She shook her head.

'I think that you have made your entirely feminine stand. Honour has been maintained. But now you want me to kiss you again.' For a second his eyes widened, like a predatory jungle cat. 'Am I right, *cara mia*?'

She stared up at him. Yes, she thought. Yes, you're right. *Kiss me.* Kiss me now. *Right now.*

He met the silent demand in her eyes and bent forwards, his mouth tracing a slow, exploratory path across her lips with the lightest of touches—barely touching her at all—which set her already racing pulse scrambling into a rapid, thready beat. The soft no-kiss kiss went on and on, until she felt that the frustration of it might kill her, but finally the tip of his tongue flicked against her, moistening her lips, and she licked at them greedily, wanting to taste him. It was more than before, but it was still not enough, and she moaned.

He raised his head then, a look of mild bemusement momentarily softening the hunger that had hardened the angles of his face as he read her expression. 'More?'

She nodded.

'Say it.'

'Yes. Yes. More. More!'

'Nice girls say please,' he said, a sudden roughness entering his voice, and this time the kiss was urgent and seeking.

Ella felt her knees grow weak, as if her bones were dissolving, and maybe he sensed it, for he caught her up and carried her into the sitting-room. He lay down on the sofa and pulled her on top of him, so that she straddled him, warm thighs clasped against his hips.

Ella closed her eyes and gave in to it. She could feel all the sinews and angles of his hard body, the hard evidence of how much he wanted her as he ground his hips against her.

'Can you feel me?' he murmured.

'Y-yes.'

He pulled her closer still. 'And now?'

Oh, God—it felt almost indecently intimate the way he was pressing himself into her, despite the barrier of their clothes. She nodded frantically as he ran his fingertip up and down the cleft of her buttocks. She felt weak and faint—disturbed by the fact that she was letting him do this to her with such apparent ease. It was as if he had cast some kind of spell on her. It was wrong, she *knew* it was wrong, and yet she didn't want to stop him. She *couldn't* stop him.

'Nico.' Her hands fluttered helplessly, her fingers briefly coiling their way through the ebony tendrils of his hair, then drifting their way down to his shoulders. Through his cool linen shirt she could feel the muscular power sheathed by silken skin, and she kneaded the flesh with rhythmical, greedy fingers. 'Nico!' she gasped.

'Nico, what?'

'Kiss me again.'

He kissed her until there were no doubts left—until she was boneless and compliant—and only then did he move his mouth away. He began to undo the buttons of her dress, one by one, and she felt the cool washing of air on her heated skin as he peeled it down over her shoulders.

His eyes darkened as he saw the peep of her breasts edging over the delicate satin and lace of her bra. 'I want to see your breasts,' he murmured possessively, stroking thoughtfully at the nipple that was peaking through the silk. 'May I?'

A dart of pleasure so fierce that it was very close to pain racked through her body. 'Y-yes.'

His hand moved to her back, to flick the hook open with almost indolent ease, and her breasts spilled out, rose-tipped and pale and magnificent. Nico felt himself grow harder still.

'And panties?' he questioned unsteadily. 'Are you wearing matching panties?'

Hadn't she put them on specially. As though she had been expecting just this? 'Yes.'

'May I see them?'

She knew what he wanted her to do. She was like a puppet, being worked by a consummate master, and she crossed her arms over her chest and pulled the dress over her head, letting it tumble unnoticed onto the floor. She heard his breathing change as his eyes drank in the indentation of her waist, the way the silk skimmed her hips and the bare thighs that straddled him, then looked at her in a way that made her feel suddenly shy. But her shyness changed into feminine pride when she saw the look of fierce and possessive hunger on his face.

He leant back a little, like a man appraising a painting, and he noted the curves and shadows of her body. The skin that had been burned by the sun had now softened to a pale golden glow, providing a creamy backdrop for the underwear. He wanted both to rip it from her and yet to make love to her while she was still wearing it. But of course it was entirely possible to indulge in both fantasies...

He moved his hand down to the camiknickers, watching the pleasured darkening of her eyes as he touched her most secret place, feeling the warm, honeyed moistness through the scrap of silk and watching the way she instinctively squirmed against his fingers.

'Nico!' she cried out.

He wanted to tell her to unzip him, was filled with a desperate longing to have her undress him as though he was any other man. But he was not, nor ever would be, and his body was his own and always would be.

He lifted her effortlessly while he rasped the zip down and impatiently kicked off his trousers and his shoes, seeing that she was now totally in his thrall as slowly and deliberately he ripped her panties, then tossed them away. He lowered her back down towards him and Ella's eyes snapped open. She looked down at him in alarm and confusion, prepared and yet unprepared as she felt the first naked nudge of him against her.

It had all happened so quickly—too quickly. Should it be this way? To make love on her sofa for the very first time, when they were still partially clothed? The blood was pounding in her ears and she quivered as she felt him pushing against her. 'Don't...don't you want to take me to bed, Nico?' she breathed.

There was something unworldly and innocent about the question, something that nagged and tugged at his conscience, as if he had broken some fundamental rule he had not been aware of.

God forgive him for plundering—for taking just what he wanted as if it was his due! And—dear God!—for forgetting to take any precautions! He bit back a groan of frustration and forced the overwhelming heat of desire to still for an instant as he lifted a hand to smooth back a sunset-coloured strand of hair.

'But I do not know where the bed is!' he bit out, in a voice made tight with tension. 'Will you show me the way, Gabriella?'

She meant to. Which was why she tried to wriggle away from him. But the movement had entirely the wrong effect, since it positioned them so that the tip of him was now inside her, and she knew that she could not move from that spot. A delicious and unstoppable warmth began to well up within her.

His eyes narrowed. 'Too late?' he guessed silkily.

Oh, much too late. 'Later,' she breathed. 'I'll show you later.'

Maybe it was just the offer of propriety she required, for now she was urging him on like there was no tomorrow. Nico could barely think straight as he reached blindly for his trousers and slid on the necessary protection. His eyes transfixed by the swaying of her breasts, he drove into her with a groan, holding onto her hips so that he could go deeper still.

'Nico!' The cry of delight was torn from her lips.

Sweet heaven! She was like a wildcat! She began to scrabble at his shirt, tearing at the buttons and whispering his name as he moved inside her, then moaning it, over and over, as if she couldn't say it enough times. He attempted to subdue her with deep, drugging kisses, but all they did was send his hunger spiralling out of control. And he was free to indulge it. Free as a lion. He had never felt this free before. Unknown and free. Just Nico.

Still lost in the rhythm, he touched her breast, feeling the nipple pucker and harden beneath his fingers and a fierce dart of pleasure threatened to take him under.

'Gabriella.'

He said her name on a shudder of broken wonder that was almost a plea, and Ella opened her eyes to stare deep into his, to see straight into his soul, into the very essence of the man himself—and that was when the pleasure engulfed her.

'Oh,' she cried softly. 'Oh. Oh. *Oh!*'

He felt himself follow her, drowning in wave upon wave of sensation, rocked and silenced by it, holding her closely, almost reverentially, until after the storm had subsided.

The muffled beat of his heart pounded a primitive rhythm and Ella lay, dazed and satiated, as she felt the steady rise and fall of his chest. It took her a few minutes to realise that he had fallen asleep, and she was glad of the moment of respite, shocked by the depth of her response to him.

She had never been so uninhibited—never, ever, ever. Absently, she dropped a kiss on the warm silken skin of his shoulder, and as he stirred lazily she turned her head slightly. The last of the setting sun's rays spilled in through the French doors, spotlighting them like two dancers as they lay sprawled and still intimately locked together on her sofa.

With an inbreath of horror she bit down on her lip, realising that she hadn't given a thought to privacy—not a thought—and that it didn't get dark until gone ten!

Why, anyone might have seen them! She might discourage casual callers, but that didn't mean they didn't come visiting. Oh, Lord. Ella felt the flush of guilt creep up to tinge her already rosy cheeks and shook Nico gently. But she couldn't resist running her fingertips over the smooth surface of his skin. He felt like silk to touch.

'Nico!' she urged softly. 'Nico! Wake up!'

Nico stirred. It was warm here, and...peaceful... yes...utterly peaceful. And that beautiful featherlight stroking. Total relaxation was such a rare and precious state for him, and he sighed and drifted back towards sleep. He didn't want to leave this place. He shook his head. 'Non!'

'Nico! Wake up! You *must*!'

The female voice drifted in and disturbed him, bringing him back to life in her arms. It was the word *must* that jarred the most. An unfamiliar word.

Nico opened his eyes to her soft pink face bent over him, her russet hair all mussed, her mouth dark from kissing, her breasts naked and soft, digging into him.

*Che cosa stava accendendo?*

It took a second or two for him to realise.

The girl from the boat! He had come to her house and then made love to her. He raised his wrist and shot a narrowed glance at his watch. Pretty fast, too.

He flicked his gaze back to her. *'Ciao, bella,'* he said softly.

Ella tensed as some indefinable quality changed him from the man who had said her name on that broken note at the height of passion. Suddenly he looked forbidding—no, maybe it was more than that. Unknown. A darkly erotic stranger she had just made love to.

'We ought to move,' she said awkwardly.

'Move?'

How stupid to feel shy after what had just happened. 'Upstairs,' she elaborated. 'To bed. Just in case…' She shrugged as she pointed towards the windows. 'Well, I would hate it if someone saw us! You know…'

Nico froze.

Oh, yes, he knew all right. He knew people who would pay countless amounts for information about just such a damaging scenario. His mouth tightened. What had he been *thinking* of? Carefully he moved her away from him and sat up, shaking his head in disbelief and anger at himself as he became fully aware of their disarranged clothing.

'Do you have a bathroom?' he asked tersely.

The bubble burst into a myriad of rainbow droplets. How dared he use that tone of voice to her? 'What do you think?' she snapped.

He saw the look of anger on her face and wanted to applaud her for not bothering to mask it behind a smile. But why should she? he asked himself. She *doesn't know who you are*!

Without warning, Ella moved off him and got to her feet, automatically reaching for her camiknickers until she remembered that he'd ripped them apart. 'I'll show you where it is,' she said furiously, 'and then you can go.'

But he was on his feet in an instant, mesmerised by the sexy thrust of her bottom, and even more by the peremptory way she was dealing with him.

He caught her by the waist and lifted her hair to nuzzle the back of her neck with the rasp of his chin. 'Do not be angry with me, Gabriella, *cara mia*.'

'Then don't *make* me angry.'

He nuzzled at her neck again. 'Am I making you angry now?' he murmured.

She shut her eyes. 'You're scratching me, actually,' she said weakly, as his chin scraped against her.

'But you like it?'

Oh, yes, she liked it all right—but then she liked just about everything he had done since he had first rung on her doorbell. And yet if she stopped to analyse it they had behaved like two...two...

She spun round to face him. 'Do you make a habit of this kind of behaviour?'

'Do you?' he countered.

'Of course I don't!'

'Well, you should,' he mused thoughtfully. 'You

really should. You are exceptionally talented at getting the very best out of a man—'

She lifted her hand to slap him, but with lightning speed he captured her wrist before it could make contact and levered her towards him.

'You dare to strike *me*?' he questioned, outraged.

She realised what she had almost done and her face crumpled. 'Oh, God, Nico—I'm sorry! I've never tried to hit a man before! Never!'

He stared at her. 'So what is it about me that makes you behave so differently?'

She shook her head distractedly. 'Maybe I'm really angry with myself—for behaving in such an outrageous manner. For letting you…. For wanting you…' she finished, in a voice that was shaking.

'For wanting me?' he echoed, and pulled her back into his arms, burying his face in her hair to hide his smile of sheer delight. 'Is that it? Is that all?'

And that really told him everything he needed to know. She liked sex; well, so did he. They had clicked in a way that was little short of dynamite, and they could click again. A beautiful, captivating woman whose appetite matched his. Two bodies in total harmony, with the added spice of distance between them that would keep hunger alive and boredom at bay. Yes, she would make a perfect lover.

Sooner or later he was going to have to reveal his identity, but he didn't anticipate a problem with that—for when had it ever been anything but the ultimate turn-on? And he would not tell her yet. For this freedom he should surely cherish while he was able to.

He reached down to pick up the crumpled and discarded dress and handed it to her, splaying the other hand proprietorially just below her belly. The tips of his fingers tangled in the damp cluster of tawny hair, and his eyes glittered with anticipation as she sucked in a shuddering and helpless breath.

'Weren't you going to show me where the bedroom is?' he drawled.

# CHAPTER SIX

THE telephone began to jangle and Ella jumped.

Let it ring, she told herself. Because if it is Nico—if *it* is—then nothing is sadder than someone who is just sitting around waiting for it to ring.

'I will call you, *cara mia*,' he had murmured, after a protracted kiss that had taken her breath away.

And then he had left, with half the buttons of his shirt missing. He had paused at the door and looked down at them, a mocking expression curving the sensual mouth. 'Good thing I'm not going straight to an appointment,' he'd murmured.

'Just where are you going?'

'To London. I have an early start.' And then, because he had needed to work out exactly how he wanted to play this, he had kissed her again. 'I'll call you.'

Up until now he hadn't. He was probably busy—at least, that was what Ella kept telling herself, trying to be cool about it, still believing that he really *would* call. Because the alternative was just too much to contemplate. That it was just a line he'd spun in order to leave without having to endure a scene. She had fallen into his arms with almost shameful ease, and maybe he'd done that typically masculine thing of wanting her and then despising what came too easily.

But it wasn't just pride that made her hope he had been telling the truth—it was the fact that she was aching to speak to him. She had believed him when they had lain there, with Nico stroking her skin, telling her that she was the most fantastic lover ever, because she had wanted to believe him—*needed* to believe him. As if that in some way justified the rampant way in which she had behaved. And the words had almost made up for the fact that he had left before midnight, with the mocking murmur of, *'Ciao, Cinderella',* ringing in her ears.

She snatched the phone up. 'Hello?'

'Ella?'

She very nearly wept and slammed it down again, for the voice was not deep and sexily foreign and she recognised it instantly, although she pretended that she hadn't.

'Speaking,' she said guardedly.

'Ella, it's Mark.'

'Oh, hello.' The frost crept into her voice quite naturally. She had hoped she'd heard the last of him, after that disastrous boat trip. 'What can I do for *you*?'

'How come you managed to avoid getting put into jail along with rest of us?' he demanded.

'I was the only one who was sober, if you remember! And I was sick.'

'So I gather.'

'Look, Mark, I'm a bit busy—'

'Not too busy to hear what I have to say.'

Ella frowned at the phone, something in his tone alerting her to trouble. 'What?'

There was a pause full of undisguised excitement.

'You know the guy who called the police?'

She couldn't let this one pass. 'You mean the man who rescued us?'

'Yeah, whatever. Well, you'll never guess what his name is?'

She didn't need to guess. She knew his name, just as she knew that his kiss had taken her to heaven and his tongue had guaranteed her a permanent place there. Ella shivered, pleasure mingling with the nagging feeling that she might never hear from him again. 'Nico,' she said. 'His name is Nico.'

'That's not his real name!'

The first feelings of foreboding began to prickle at her skin. 'What are you talking about?'

'His real name is Nicolo!'

'So he abbreviates it,' said Ella coldly. 'Lots of people do. I do. So what?'

'Nicolo of Mardivino,' he emphasised carefully.

She still didn't get it. 'Yes, that's where he lives.'

'*Prince* Nicolo!' he declared triumphantly.

'Mark, have you been drinking again?' But even as she asked the question the import of his words finally struck home, and Ella very nearly dropped the phone. '*What* did you say?' she hissed.

'He's a prince!'

'Of course he isn't! He's... He's...' But her words

tailed off, instinct telling her she had to believe the unbelievable. But sometimes you fought instinct when it told you something you didn't want to hear. 'I don't believe it.'

'Check it up, then! He's the youngest Prince—there's three of them! Bit of a playboy, as you'd expect.' He gave a crude laugh. 'A daredevil and a ladies' man!'

Ella's fingers bit into the receiver. 'Was there anything else, Mark?'

A sly note was injected into his voice. 'So just what happened after we'd gone? Did you sleep with him?'

Ella slammed the phone down with a shaking hand.

Of course he wasn't a prince! Princes didn't rescue you and nurse you and then turn up at your front door and...

And make love to you.

Scarcely aware of what she was doing, she went straight back to her computer and tapped the words 'Mardivino + Prince Nicolo' into a search engine, licking her dry lips in horror as she saw that there were 36,700 entries. She clicked onto the first one and waited for what seemed like an eternity, until suddenly there it was—a picture of Nico who, it seemed, was not just Nico at all, but His Serene Highness Prince Nicolo Louis Fantone Cacciatore.

There were details about his schooling, in Mardivino and France and Italy, and pictures of him with his family—except that this particular family happened to be sitting in a throne room decked with ornate gold and precious jewels.

Ella honestly thought she was going to be sick.

The powerful car nosed its way like a silver predator along the narrow lanes and once again Nico glanced into his driving mirror, but the road behind him was still empty.

Should he have rung her?

No, better this way. Face to face and person to person.

He was clever with words and good with women. He would explain why he hadn't told her and make her understand. And then he would kiss her again, in a way guaranteed to have her forgive him anything.

He felt the deep ache of desire, tempered only marginally by his awareness that their lovemaking had been too…

The dark brows knitted. Too what? Too intimate? Intimacy was dangerous and misleading and to be avoided. It weakened you and it gave women expectations. Expectations that could never be met—particularly for someone like Ella.

But she had been everything. Tender. Passionate. Warm. Provocative. And maybe the most potent of all those had been the tenderness, because for Nico it was an unknown quantity. He never allowed people close enough for tenderness, and he hadn't been expecting it. It had crept up on him unawares—like the feeling of gentle torpor after just a mouthful of especially good wine.

Maybe it was because he hadn't felt the need—or *had* the need—to put up the usual barriers to protect himself. For once he had been able to pretend that he was just anyone, and she had responded to him with a passion that had taken him unawares.

And he wanted more of that passion.

He parked in the lane leading up to her cottage and slowly locked the car, pocketing the keys thoughtfully, aware of the lush green froth of the leaves on the trees and the sunshine that dappled the dusty ground. He could hear the sweet, soaring sound of birdsong and that surprised him, too—had his senses suddenly come alive?

It's just the power of new and different sex, he told himself. His appetite had been jaded and she had simply been something fresh on his tastebuds. And, oh, how he wanted to taste her again…

He rang the doorbell.

Standing out of view in the kitchen, Ella heard the bell above her thundering heart and thought about ignoring it. Surely that would be best? Presumably he would go away and that would be that. She couldn't see him standing waiting patiently all day—because that wasn't the kind of thing that princes did, was it?

But if she let him walk away then there would be no sense of closure. Realistically, she knew their paths would never cross again and she would never get the opportunity to say what she wanted to say. Or rather, to tell him what he *needed* to hear. The conniving, deceiving *snake*!

How would he be expecting her to react?

It nearly killed her, but Ella fixed a look of delighted surprise on her face as she pulled open the door. Well, even that wasn't completely false. He might have deceived her, but that didn't stop her responding to him on a purely physical level.

And as a man, he was utterly magnificent. The endlessly long, muscular legs were encased in dark faded denim, and he wore a black T-shirt that clung to every sinew of his impressive torso. His black hair was ruffled, as if he had been driving with the roof down, and his dark eyes were set like precious jewels in his olive skin.

But the thought of jewels made her remember, and she only just stopped herself from slamming the door shut again.

'Nico!' she breathed, in what she hoped was the manner of a smitten woman talking to her new lover. 'I wasn't expecting you!'

'I should have rung.'

She let the mildest reproach enter her voice. 'Well, you *did* say you would.'

He unconsciously relaxed, the tension leaving his body as he acknowledged the undramatic greeting. So she didn't know! Which meant, of course, that he was going to have to tell her.

But not yet.

Later…

First let him have one more heart-stopping after-noon of unburdened lovemaking in her arms. 'May I come in?'

For a moment Ella's nerve almost left her. It would be easier and less distracting if she told him here, now. And then she steeled herself. Surely she wasn't so weak and wimpish that she would let his overpowering presence influence her in the light of what she had discovered?

She set her mouth into a glassy smile. Such a prac-tised master of deceit! Let Prince Nicolo of Mardivino have a taste of his own medicine!

'Of course,' she said lightly, and whirled off to-wards the kitchen, leaving him to follow her. 'Come through.'

Nico frowned, because now he really *was* sur-prised. Surely this time she *should* have melted into his arms? Was she regretting what had happened? Deciding that maybe it had been too easy last time? The frown became a smile as he acknowledged yet another facet of this unknown world. He could wait...it would do him good to wait...and the waiting would fuel his already sharpened appetite.

She was standing beside the fridge, looking as if she was starring in an old-fashioned commercial, with a bright smile on her face.

'What can I get you, Nico? Champagne?'

He began to grow uneasy. They had been to bed, yes, and it had been pretty damned wonderful—but it was hardly a cause for celebration, was it? He racked back through his memory, trying to recall what he had said to her in those incredible few hours in bed. No, nothing to give her the idea that this wasn't anything other than a brief affair.

'Do *you* want champagne?' he questioned.

And Ella knew then that she could not maintain this façade a moment longer. 'Actually, I think it would choke me.'

His eyes narrowed. 'Then why did you—'

'But that's probably because it's fairly ordinary champagne.' She cut right through his words, noting his fleeting look of surprise. He probably wasn't used to *that*, she surmised. People *interrupting* him. 'And I expect you're used to drinking only the finest stuff, aren't you? *Nicolo.*'

His heart beat with the dull, heavy thud of something that felt a little like disappointment—if only he was sure how that felt. But one thing he was sure of was his own stupidity. He had been living in a fantasy all of his own making. 'You know?' he said dully.

'Yes.'

Of course she knew. His thoughts whirled round like a child's spinning wheel. When? When she had opened her eyes after her fever? Or even before that? Maybe she had known all along. Maybe he had completely misjudged her and she was an avid reader of those tacky tabloid newspapers that delighted in printing snatched photographs of him.

Maybe she hadn't been able to believe her luck

when she had opened her eyes to discover just who it was who had rescued her.

Had all this been planned and his first instinct the right one? That she was nothing more than a beautiful decoy, groomed to capture a prince? His body tensed. 'When did you find out?'

With a mounting sensation of disbelief she stared at him, hearing the cold shot of accusation in his voice. 'When do you *think*?'

Now he began to wonder whether their innocent and frantic coupling on the sofa had not been so innocent, after all. What if there *had* been photographers lurking in the undergrowth? Photographs now in existence that might now find their way onto some sick home-movie site on the Internet? The realisation of just how foolhardy he had been made his blood run cold.

'I don't know,' he said icily. 'That's why I'm asking.'

She had gone in on the attack and now she felt stung to defence. How dared he? How *dare* he? 'You think I knew all along, don't you?'

He hid his turbulent thoughts behind the icy mask that was second nature to him. 'Did you?'

Her eyes opened very wide. 'And you think that's why I went to bed with you?'

'Was it?'

If she had thought that she felt sick before, then nausea had just entered a whole new dimension. He could think *that* of her?

But why shouldn't he? She had behaved like a tramp! She had nearly slapped him before, but she could not and would not attempt to do so again. Why, in the light of what she now knew, he might have her arrested for some kind of treason!

The truth came babbling out of her mouth like a hotspring. 'I didn't have a clue who you were, if you must know! I thought you were just some guy who worked for a rich man.' Her eyes shot emerald fire at him. 'Why wouldn't I? Princes aren't exactly thick on the ground.'

He realised that he had wounded her with his stubborn, arrogant pride. He wished he could take the words back, but he couldn't, and so instead he moved towards her, his hands outstretched in a gesture of peace. 'Gabriella—'

'The name I use,' she said furiously, 'is Ella—just as yours is Nicolo. That's the reality. And the two people who made the mistake of getting close were not real. You were playing out some sort of fantasy, so let's just leave it at that, shall we?'

Her perception rocked him almost as much as the certain knowledge that this was something his easy charm could not fix. Not if the raging look on her face was anything to go by.

'What if I told you that I didn't want to leave it?' he questioned softly.

Her answering look was contemptuous. 'Presumably you've spent your whole life getting exactly what you want?'

He had the grace to shrug.

'Well, this time you're not! I want you to go now, and I don't want ever to see you again.' She sucked in a hot, dry breath, afraid that she might do something regrettable—like burst into noisy tears of humiliation. Far worse than the crushing realisation that he had led her on—fooled her with some game of make-believe—was the hurt she felt inside. She had been blown away by him, she had given him something of her heart as well as her body, and now there must be painful surgery to reclaim that little piece of her heart. 'Because I don't enjoy being made a fool of.'

Damn her for her insolence! For daring to talk to him in this way! He should turn on his heel, walk away and forget all about her. 'That is what you want?' he asked in a low voice.

'Shall I say it in French?' she mocked. 'Or Italian? Or Spanish? Will that help you understand a little better?'

Her anger had loosened her up enough so that he was able to take her off guard, whispering the tips of his fingers down over the silken surface of her cheek and noting the immediate tremble of her lips, the darkening of her eyes, with a strange and heady triumph.

For it was second nature to him to fight for what he wanted—to prove to himself that he was capable of getting it on his own merits, and not by relying on the entitlements that accompanied a mere accident of birth.

'*Muy bien,*' he murmured, lapsing instinctively into the tongue spoken by his ancestors—Spanish Conquistadors who had fought so long and so hard for Mardivino. 'I will leave you now, Gabriella, and you can reflect on your folly at leisure. For folly it is.' His eyes glittered with the light of battle. 'You are fighting a battle with yourself for no reason, because you still want me as much as I want you.'

'You really *are* living in fantasy land!' she declared witheringly.

The heat of desire beat through him. 'You will be mine again,' he promised silkily, crushing her fingers to his lips before turning on his heel and slamming his way out of the house.

# CHAPTER SEVEN

ELLA stared at the letter as if it was contaminated.

'You don't seem very *excited*,' observed Rachel, her own eyes shining. 'I mean, most people would be jumping up and down to get a Royal request!' She picked up the letter again and read it as reverentially as if it had been a Dead Sea Scroll. 'I just can't believe it! A letter from the Mardivinian Bureau of Tourism,' she repeated wonderingly. 'Asking us for our professional advice!'

Ella sighed and she gave her assistant a weak smile. Rachel was young and enthusiastic, but those very qualities—which had led Ella to employ her in the first place—were also those that would make it difficult for her to understand why she had no intention of accepting this job. Though when she stopped to think about it what could she say to *anyone* that would make the facts believable?

How about if she just blurted it out? She could just imagine how the conversation would go.

*Actually, it's just a ruse to get me to go to Mardivino, Rachel.*

*And why is that, Ella?*

*Well, the Prince rescued me from a stricken boat, only I didn't know he was a prince at the time. He subsequently came here for dinner and I slept with him, and when I discovered that he had deceived me I told him I never wanted to see him again.*

She chose her words carefully. Perhaps professional concern might be more advisable. 'To be honest, Rachel, I'm not sure if I can spare the time to go,' she prevaricated.

Rachel stared at her as if she had gone stark, raving mad. 'But I can handle the office here—you know I can!' A hurt expression came over her face. 'Unless, of course, you don't think I'm capable of running the office—though you've let me do it before!'

'Of course I don't think that!'

Rachel was shaking her head. 'I mean—this is like something out of a fairy tale!'

Maybe it was, thought Ella—but not in the way that Rachel meant. It was certainly like the part in the stories where the apple you bit sent you into a century-long sleep, or where your glass carriage became a pumpkin. The dark side of the fairy story...

'It could turn out to be a bigger project than a small firm like ours can handle.'

Rachel lifted her hands in a gesture that said, *So what?* 'If it's too big, then we just take on more staff!'

Ella stared at her assistant as an idea slowly began to take shape. A solution that would not just save her skin, but thrill Rachel into the bargain. And one that Prince Nicolo Louis Fantone Cacciatore couldn't possibly object to...

'Do you want to go down to the village and buy some bread for our lunch?' she said innocently.

As soon as Rachel had gone, Ella picked up the thick sheet of cream paper with the heavily embossed crest at the top and dialled a number with a shaking finger, hardly able to believe that it would get her straight through to the palace at Mardivino.

But it did, and she very nearly dropped the receiver when she heard the rich, silky voice. *'Si? Nicolo.'*

So how did she address him now? As Nico, or Nicolo, or Prince, or—perhaps most appropriate of all—as *rat*!

'Nico?' she said coolly, without any kind of formality.

Within the quiet, opulent splendour of his palace office, Nico could feel the deep, dark throb of his pulse as he heard her voice. As he had known he would. *'Ciao, Gabriella,'* he said silkily. 'Did you get my letter?'

'How else do you think I knew your number?' she questioned coldly.

His pulse quickened further. He was a man who constantly sought new adventures, and he had never before realised what a turn-on insolence could be. 'So when will you be arriving?' he enquired pleasantly.

Oh, but her reply was going to give her such great delight! A tiny revenge, it was true—but an empowering one, which would go a little way towards healing some of the hurt and humiliation she felt. 'I won't be. I'll be sending my assistant instead.'

There was a pause. 'Oh, no, you won't,' he said softly.

She ignored the silken threat in his voice. 'She's very capable—and this will be a wonderful opportunity for her!'

'But it is not your assistant that I want, *cara*—it is you.'

Despot! Well, he had better learn that she was *not* one of his subjects, and he couldn't just dictate to her as if she was. 'I think it's time I enlightened you, *Prince* Nicolo. Point one—it is pretty pathetic to invent a job just because you want to see someone again, especially when she has no desire to see you— ever! And, point two—either my assistant comes or you can kiss the "job" goodbye.'

He gave a low laugh, curling his long fingers around the phone in an instinctive movement of delicious anticipation. She was just crying out to be conquered, as he had conquered mountains and oceans ever since he could remember.

'Point one, Gabriella—your ego may be vast enough to regard this as simply a ploy, but my need for your services is genuine.'

'Oh, really?' she questioned disbelievingly.

'Yes, really.' He stared reflectively out at the sapphire sweep of the sea. 'Mardivino is a small island which needs to overhaul its tourist industry selectively. Its popularity is growing, and we have all seen the dangers of that elsewhere. When too many people come there is a risk that the original charm of a place will be destroyed. It is happening here, and it is happening now.'

'That isn't really my end of the market at all,' she said coolly.

'Then perhaps it should be,' he returned. 'I have had your company thoroughly investigated and I like what you do. I like it very much.'

'Actually, I'm not looking for your approval, Nico.' But she might as well not have spoken for all the notice he took.

'Sometimes a relatively untutored eye can see what all the so-called "experts" cannot—you have both vision and imagination, Gabriella, and that is what I am looking for.'

'Oh, hoist the flag! Declare a national holiday! Am I supposed to be pleased? Because I'm not! I never sought your approval and—'

'And point two,' he said, his words cutting through her protestation like steel lancing through soft flesh. 'Please understand that I mean what I say. I do not want your assistant. I want you.'

'Well, that's tough! I'm not coming!'

The fight and her resistance was tantalising him to an unbearable pitch, but the tone of his voice remained clipped and emphatic. 'I think that you will. Or rather, that you should. I am not used to having my requests turned down, and if you refuse then I am afraid that your business might…. How shall I put this?' There was another pause. 'You might discover that there has been a sudden downturn in your fortunes.'

Quiet menace underpinned his words, and with a chilling certainty Ella knew that he spoke the truth. She didn't know how he could damage her business, she just knew that he *could*. 'Are you…are you *threatening* me?' she demanded incredulously.

'It is all a matter of perception, surely?' he answered softly. 'I am merely offering you a wonderful opportunity, one that it would be exceedingly foolish of you to turn down. It would be professional suicide,' he finished.

He was a clever and perceptive man—damn him! For someone whose position must mean that he was largely protected from the world and all its problems, he knew about the value of a job like this. Or had he grown up knowing that he could have everything he wanted—just so long as the price was right?

Ella injected frost into her voice. At least that way she could stop it from trembling with rage. 'And if I accept? If I do the job which you say you have for me—do I have your word that you will leave me alone?'

'But I deal with tourism on the island,' he said innocently. 'It would make no sense at all for me to make a promise that I cannot keep, *cara*. You will, of course, have to *liaise* with me.'

He managed to make the word sound indecently sexual—which, presumably, had been his intention. And her impotent rage did not protect her from the sudden shimmering of sensation over her skin as she remembered with erotic clarity just how accomplished a lover he was.

'I think we're talking at cross-purposes here, Nico,' she said softly. 'And as for promises—I can make one that I have every intention of keeping, and that is that you will not get what it is you want.'

'But you do not know what that is, do you, Gabriella?' he mocked.

No, but she had a pretty good idea. She wasn't stupid, nor was she completely inexperienced. She hadn't been a virgin. There had been a couple of lovers in her past, but none of them had come even close to matching Nico. It was about so much more than technique—it had been as though she had never really made love properly before. With him it had been an experience that transcended anything she had ever felt in the arms of another man.

He had made it seem as if her body was boneless, weightless, melding with his as if it had been born to do only that. She had felt her heart beating beneath him and the hard heat of his body within hers. In his arms she had been helpless and yet powerful—and she had seen his face soften with a pleasure and a joy that had only added to her own. And they had tasted those pleasures for only one fleeting night—of course he would want to experience it all over again. Heaven only knew, just thinking about it now was enough to set her own body aching.

But things had changed. Even if he hadn't deceived

her—*which he had*—the relative innocence of what had happened between them could never be recreated. He was not who she had thought he was. He had kept his identity secret—and as secrets went it was a pretty big one.

Was his persistence due to the fact that she had sent him packing and that had never happened before in his privileged life? What other reason would he have for twisting her arm to fly to his island?

Well, he was in for a big surprise. Ella's family had often accused her of stubbornness, and she knew that it could sometimes be a fault, but at a time like now it was going to prove very useful indeed—although she would prefer to define it as resolve.

'So you are agreed, Gabriella?' the soft, mocking voice prompted her.

She briefly thought about appealing to his better nature—but she could hear his steely determination. She thought about calling his bluff. Would he really go through with something as hostile as ruining her tiny company simply because she would not accede to his will? Might he not just shrug those broad, hard shoulders and accept what she wanted with something approaching good grace? There must, after all, be literally hundreds of other women who would leap to be his lover.

No.

Instinct told her that he was used to getting what he wanted—and he wanted her. Well, he could have her—but only on her terms.

'Very well. I accept.'

'Excellent.'

She could hear the triumph in his voice and clenched her free hand into a little fist. Oh, why hadn't she slapped him properly when she had had the opportunity? She breathed in deeply, forcing herself to sound cool. 'But first I need a little more information about precisely what it is I am expected to do.'

'I think that will be a little easier when you are here. You shall have all the information you need.'

She ignored that. 'That's not good enough, Nico,' she said sweetly. 'I'd like you to fax me some statistics about numbers of tourists, their accommodation requirements and so on—can you please arrange that for me as soon as possible?'

Even at school he hadn't been spoken to in such a stern and bossy way! He should feel righteous indignation at her insubordination, and yet he had never heard anything quite so tantalising in his life. How great the pleasure would be of subduing her with the skilful touch of his lips! And if statistics were what it took to fly her out to Mardivino, then she could have all the damned statistics she wanted! Staring out of the palace window at the intense blue of the sea, Nico gave a slow and predatory smile. 'Very well.'

'I will fly out at the beginning of next week.'

'Tell me when and I will arrange a plane. In fact,' he added, on a low note of delight, 'I will fly you to Mardivino myself.'

Now there was triumph in *her* voice. 'Oh, no, you won't, Nico,' she said softly. 'Once was enough!'

'You are criticising my flying ability?'

'No, I am resisting your efforts to control me. You want my expertise and you'll get it, but you will be treated in exactly the same way as any other client. There will be no preferential treatment—not for you, and certainly not for me. I will take a scheduled airline flight, thank you very much, and I will add the cost to my bill.'

For a moment he was speechless, scarcely able to believe what he was hearing. She was refusing his offer! To be flown openly to Mardivino by the youngest Prince of that principality!

'Oh, and one more thing, Nico?'

She was making *more* requests? Through the haze of disbelief and thwarted desire he felt a glimmer of reluctant admiration for her tenacity and guts. 'Go on.'

'I trust that my accommodation requirements will be totally above board? I will require a room for me, and for me alone, and if you renege on that I will take the first available flight home and you really will have to find someone else.'

'Very well,' he said coldly. 'And now I will give you the number of my mobile.'

'Go on, then.'

He had never felt so frustrated. Did she not realise the honour he was according her—giving her access to him whenever she wanted? He had been about to tell her not to abuse the privilege, but now his lips snapped closed. Clearly she didn't even see it as a privilege!

'*Jusque là, cherie,*' he murmured.

Momentarily she was confused by the sudden switch in language. 'I thought you usually used Italian?'

He watched a speedboat sweeping across the bay. 'It depends. Italian is the language of love—although my French and Spanish cousins would disagree—and I am not feeling particularly *loving* towards you at the moment, Gabriella.'

She couldn't let this one pass. Oh, no. 'I think you're in danger of confusing love with sex, Nico,' she said quietly, and put the phone down.

# CHAPTER EIGHT

'AND just *where* are you proposing she stay, Nicolo?'

'At the palace, of course.'

'No.' Gianferro's voice was flat and unequivocal. 'I will not tolerate one of your mistresses staying here in the Palace.'

Nico didn't react. Not straight away. Over the years he had learnt that considered argument was better than a hot-headed blaze of outrage—especially with his eldest brother. Biting back his words went against his nature but he had learned to school himself in diplomacy when dealing with Gianferro. For Gianferro was the heir. The glittering eldest son over whom the double-edged sword of leadership hung by only a whisper, since their father, the King, had lain sick in his palace suite for many months now.

In a way, Gianferro had both the best and the worst of the Royal world—the heady aphrodisiac of power, coupled with the stultifying burden of responsibility. The eldest son was seen as the most privileged, but Nico knew that despite how the outside world perceived it, there was no such thing as the perfect position in a Royal family of three brothers.

Guido, the middle brother, was currently living abroad—and middle brothers were notoriously touchy about being looked over and ignored. Even in so-called *normal* families they had difficulty establishing a legitimate role. It explained why he had left Mardivino as quickly as he could, making for himself the comfortable life of international playboy.

Nico, as the youngest, should by rights have been the spoilt baby of the family—except things had not turned out that way.

His very birth had heralded the illness that had killed his mother—and ever after his father's pride in him had always been tempered by sadness and melancholy.

Gianferro had almost stepped into the role of father—if such a thing was possible when the age gap was only seven years. He had always looked out for and fiercely protected Nico, and as the years had passed had been reluctant to lose that role of mentor. Nico had had to fight every bit of the way for independence.

'Gabriella is not my mistress,' he stated flatly.

'Oh, really?' Gianferro raised dark, disbelieving brows. 'Is this not the same flame-haired woman whom you took to the beach house? The consort of the drunks who spent the night in Solajoya jail?'

Nico stared at him. 'You knew about that?'

'But of course I knew. The Chief of Police rang to inform me of what was happening.'

'He gossips like an old woman,' said Nico darkly.

Gianferro laughed. 'He simply does his job. I know everything that happens on Mardivino, and it is my duty to do so—particularly when it concerns my brothers. And a mistress staying here at the palace would wreck your reputation—in the same way that one of those crazy sports you indulge in will soon wreck your life.'

Nico sighed. It was as pointless as whistling in the wind to attempt to defend his lifestyle. He had tried often enough over the years.

Just as it would be pointless to try to explain that nothing had happened between him and Gabriella at the beach. Given Nico's past catalogue of lovers, Gianferro simply would not believe him. And even if the truth *were* known—would that not offend his innate masculine pride and reputation?

'Are you *forbidding* it, Gianferro?' Nico questioned, in a voice that was only half joking.

'No.' Gianferro gave an answering glimmer of a smile which briefly softened his hard mouth. 'I am simply appealing to your sense of what is proper and what is not, Nico.'

'You know she is here on a legitimate assignment?' Nicolo said casually. 'She works in the travel industry.'

'How very convenient for you both.' There was a pause. 'And what precisely is she proposing to do here on the island?'

There was a brief pause, and Nico saw the dark light of challenge in his brother's eyes. He kept his counsel. 'I'll keep you posted,' he said lightly.

Gianferro gave a low laugh. 'Give her an office

here at the palace, then, but put her up in L'Etoile.
That should be luxurious enough to impress her.'

'You think that is what I am trying to do?'

The brothers' eyes met.

'I do not know what it is that you are trying to do,
but I know you well enough to guess,' said Gianferro
softly. 'I understand that she is beautiful, and that
speaks for itself—but never forget that for a man in
your position she can never be anything more than a
sensual diversion, Nico.'

Nicolo's lips curved in a cynical smile. 'I need no
warnings from you, Gianferro,' he retorted softly.
'And to me she has never been anything *but* a sensual
diversion.'

Ella's journey to Mardivino might have been on a
scheduled flight for a national airline, but there all
similarity to other air travel ended.

She had taken the earliest possible flight, and was
fussed over and waited on like a heavily pregnant
woman about to give birth. She doubted whether the
other first-class passengers were being treated with
quite so much regard. Was that because Nico—*Prince
Nicolo*—had arranged for her to come?

She got a sudden disturbing glimpse of what it
must be like to be him—with everyone always on
their best behaviour and pandering to your every
need. Was he ever able to have 'normal' interaction
with people? she wondered. Probably not. And that
couldn't be good for you.

Her lips tightened. It definitely wasn't. It could make you into a control freak—as he had just demonstrated. He had got her here by sheer and arrogant force of will. Had his whole life been spent doing exactly that?

His deception still hurt, but her inner sense of unease came from more than that. She had fallen into his arms and made love to him in a way that had been new and exciting and precious. But he had trampled on all those feelings with his duplicity. And if he had done it to her once, then he could do it again. A man in Nico's position would not care about a woman's feelings—why should he? Willing sexual partners were probably lining up halfway round the block for him.

She must keep her head and dampen down any dangerous see-sawing emotions every time they threatened to appear. Try to keep things in perspective. It had been great sex, that was all. She must not learn to care for him because nothing would come of it—nothing *could* come of it.

And you *are* a strong woman, she reminded herself. You know you are. Of course you can resist him.

Landing at Solajoya Airport was a dream—with no Customs or queues to get through. She was first off the flight and met on the tarmac by Nico himself, and despite everything she had vowed her heart began to race as he made his way towards her.

'Hello, Gabriella,' he said softly.

'I...I wasn't expecting you to come and meet me

in person,' she stumbled, because the impact of seeing him here unexpectedly had blown away most of her good intentions. Where was the strong woman now?

He gave a half smile. 'You thought I would send a servant, perhaps?'

'Something like that.'

'Well, I have put myself in that role.' His black eyes glittered. 'And I am at your service, *cara*.'

She thought that he'd managed to make it sound like an erotic declaration. 'Does that mean you will docilely agree to all my orders?' she asked, as he opened the boot of the car.

He turned to look at her, a mocking yet serious light playing at the back of his eyes. 'But you must treat your servants with respect,' he said softly. 'Or they will not respect you.'

*And what about your lovers?* she wanted to ask. *How much do you respect them?*

Yet as he took her bag from her and slung it into the boot of a low black limousine Ella couldn't resist the forbidden luxury of running her eyes over him.

She had seen him looking like a beachcomber, and as a coolly elegant European, but today he was unmistakably a prince. There was something about the way his suit was cut that, even to Ella's untutored eye, made it look about as costly as it was possible to be. His shirt was of palest blue and finest silk, unbuttoned at the neck to show a sprinkling of dark hair.

*And I have seen him naked,* Ella thought, with a

sudden debilitating rush of pride and longing. *I have held him in my arms while he thrust long and hard and deep within me.*

Yeah, you and a million others, mocked the cynical voice of reason. But reason did nothing to prevent an aching heart.

Nico turned round and frowned. 'Your cheeks are flushed, *cara*,' he said quietly. 'And your eyes are troubled—why is that?'

She buried the desire and regret, and lifted her chin in an attitude of pride. 'Why do you think, Nico? Could it have anything to do with the fact that I have been forced to accept this assignment against my better judgement? Blackmailed and threatened to do your bidding?'

Not quite, he thought wryly. Or she would be sending him a message of eager anticipation, not this outrageous defiance. 'And you are going to sulk about it for the duration of your stay?'

'Absolutely not. I intend to do the job I am being paid for to the very best of my ability. You asked me a question and I answered it. But if my "troubled" expression offends the Prince, then I shall replace it with a smile!' She fixed him with a bright and mocking curve of her lips. 'Is that better, Nico? Is that what you're used to?'

Nico's eyes narrowed. He had been expecting— what? That she would be secretly happy to be whisked back here to the island? That her protests were the kind that women sometimes made when they wanted something but knew that it was perhaps political not to show it? Now he was not so sure. And uncertainty was a feeling he was not familiar with.

'Let's go,' he said tightly, and held the door of the car open for her.

With Nico behind the wheel they sped out of the tiny airport, waved through and bowed to by guards. A group of people who were milling around by the exit, waiting at a taxi-rank, spotted their car and began pointing at it. One or two even started waving and shooting cameras in their direction!

Ella blinked in bemusement. 'Is it always like this?'

Nico gave a rather brittle smile. 'You ain't seen nothing yet.'

'That's rather a good American accent,' she observed.

'So it should be—I went to college there.'

'Whereabouts?'

'Stanford.'

Had she somehow thought that he had spent all his life on the island? An American education would go a long way towards explaining his easy, cosmopolitan attitude. 'And did you like it?' she questioned curiously.

He smiled. 'Loved it. But I was young then,' he said mockingly.

How little she really knew of him. She had thought that it was the big things that were important—his Royal status for starters—but in a crystal-clear moment of perception she realised that it was all the tiny things that provided the building blocks for understanding a person. People were complex, and none more than this dark, handsome figure beside her.

She remembered him telling her that he dealt with tourism on the island, and this was something she needed to know about. 'So, do you actually have a *job*?'

His smile was cynical. 'Did you imagine I'd sit around on a throne all day and be waited on?'

'Something like that,' she admitted, with a shrug. 'Sorry. Tell me a bit about it—I'd like to know.'

Genuine interest was pretty hard to resist, he was discovering—but wasn't there more to it than that? Didn't he want in some way to redeem himself in her eyes? To show her that he wasn't just some lazy dilettante with no real function, commitment, or purpose?

'I've been concentrating on hauling the city of Solajoya out of the past and trying to regenerate it,' he said slowly. 'Its size and location are pretty much perfect for the media and software industries.'

'So it would rely on more than banks and tax exiles?'

'You've done your homework,' he remarked.

'Please don't patronise me, Nico!'

'I wasn't,' he said, in a voice that was almost gentle. 'I was applauding your work ethic, if you must know.'

She didn't want to bask in his praise, like a cat sitting in front of a glowing fire, she wanted to remain immune to him—all of him. But she could see it wasn't going to be easy.

She settled back in her seat and stared out of the window. The sky was as blue as a swimming pool, and the sun beat down on the magenta blooms of the trees that lined the roads. She was filled with the sudden sense of exhilaration that a new and beautiful place always gave her—until she reminded herself of the reason why she was here. *Pretend he isn't twenty-eight and devastatingly gorgeous and virile. He's an old man. A grandfather.* 'So which is the *official* language of Mardivino?' she asked politely, because her reference books hadn't made this very clear.

He increased the speed of the car, a slight smile playing at the corners of his mouth. More homework, he guessed. 'The four languages of Italian, Spanish, French and English are interchangable,' he said.

'But isn't that very confusing?'

'Not for me,' he said softly. 'For a linguist it is extremely useful. It means that you are rarely at the disadvantage of not being able to understand what is being said.' His eyes gleamed. 'It also means that you can switch language so that people do not always understand *you*.'

Ella snorted. 'Well, if I were you I would brush up on your interpretation skills, Nico! Because I distinctly remember telling you that I didn't want to take this job, and yet you still twisted my arm to get me here!'

He laughed softly. 'Ah, Gabriella—do you not

know that a man finds it unbearably exciting when a woman spars with him the way that you do?'

'Particularly when he's not used to it?' she queried perceptively.

'Especially that,' he agreed. Why, meeting such defiance and insubordination head-on was almost like learning a new language in itself!

'That isn't why I'm doing it,' she objected.

'I know it isn't. Now, let's call a truce for the moment. You are here, and you might as well enjoy it, so why don't you look out of the window again and you can see how beautiful my island is?'

'Where are we going?' she asked suddenly.

'You will be staying at L'Etoile Hotel,' he replied. 'You have heard of it, perhaps?'

Of course she had—she had spent the past few days learning as much as she could about the principality— and for a small island it had a hell of a lot of history. L'Etoile was the kind of hotel that vied with the world's finest for style and luxury and elegance. The kind of place whose prices were beyond the reach of ordinary mortals.

With mounting dismay Ella stared down at her rather rumpled skirt. Wasn't she going to stand out like a very sore thumb?

You're in the travel business, she reminded herself. No one will be expecting you to compete with the jet-set.

'That should be fun,' she said evenly.

'And you will work from a small office within the palace,' he said casually.

Ella swallowed. If she had thought her clothes too ordinary for a luxury hotel, then how the hell was she going to compete in a *palace*? You won't, she told herself. You'll just be yourself.

'Could you drive me through as much of the main town as possible on the way there?' she asked coolly.

'Any particular reason why?'

'I just want to get the lie of the land. The more I know, the better prepared I will be.' *And the sooner I can get home again.* But her attention was caught by a cluster of gleaming white buildings that suddenly made home seem a very long way away.

'We're just coming into Solajoya now. I'll take you by the backstreets.'

And it was beautiful, thought Ella as she looked down. Utterly beautiful. The roads were narrow and winding, with tall shuttered houses decked with pots of brightly coloured flowers.

He negotiated steep curves towards what was obviously the centre, where the main streets were thronged with people—some clearly heading back from the beach, while others were clustered outside a large, white building, creating a kind of human bottleneck. There were long-haired students in jeans sitting on the steps to the building, writing postcards, and earnest-looking older groups, all studying guidebooks with rapt preoccupation.

Ella leaned forward. 'What's going on in there?'

'It is the gallery of Juan Lopez,' explained Nico. 'You know him?'

Ella frowned. 'He's an artist?' she remembered.

'Was. He died over fifty years ago—an early and tragic death—but for an artist that is always a good selling point.'

'How cynical!' observed Ella.

'How true,' he retorted softly.

'Tell me about him.'

He smiled, realising that their relationship had been forged in relative equality, and that she had no intention of tempering her attitude towards him now, in the light of what she had since discovered.

'He was what they call "an artist's artist"—a student of Picasso, and he lived most of his life here. Those who know him love him, and come from all over the world to see his work. He bequeathed it all to Mardivino, on condition that it stay here. He loved this island, you see.'

And, looking out at the distant harbour, Ella could see exactly why. It was like a toy town—the buildings all pure white, the main street lined with palm trees that swayed gently in the breeze.

The car approached the sea and suddenly there was L'Etoile—white against the sapphire backdrop, and glittering as starrily as its name implied.

Nico stopped the car outside and turned to look at her, and Ella's breath caught in her throat. It was okay in theory to tell yourself that you were going to be immune to a man's charisma, but quite another when

you were confronted with it in such close proximity—
so close that you could almost feel the warmth of his
breath, almost touch the silken texture of his olive
skin, see for yourself the black, glittering eyes that
both mocked and enticed.

'You have a choice, *cara*,' he said softly. 'I can
accompany you inside, if you prefer, but if I do there
will be something of a…a *fuss*,' he concluded, after
a moment.

She remembered the people pointing at him at the
airport, how he must live his life with a sense of being
continually on show. 'Do you go to that beach hut to
escape all the *fuss*?' she questioned, momentarily forgetting that she was supposed to be keeping this trip
on a purely professional footing.

'But of course. It is peaceful and isolated there.'
The corners of his mouth lifted in a lazy smile. 'Bar
the odd mermaid washed up on my shore, of course.'

'Then please don't come inside,' she said quickly,
but it was less to do with the projected 'fuss' than the
dangers of that achingly soft smile.

He nodded and glanced at his watch. 'Okay, I'll
leave you to unpack your stuff.'

'I haven't brought very much. I don't intend to stay
here longer than a week, Nico.'

His eyes glittered. She would stay here for as long
as *he* deemed it necessary—no more and no less. 'I'll
pick you up in an hour,' he said steadily. 'Show you
your office at the palace.'

'Make it two. I want to wander round on my own

for a bit first. Get a feel for the place before I enter the hallowed portals of the palace.'

'I will have someone accompany you.'

'You will not! I want to be free to explore on my own.'

*Free*, he thought, with a sudden sense of yearning. 'You are a very stubborn woman, Gabriella,' he said softly.

'I don't deny it.'

He opened his mouth to object, and then shut it again—for what could he do? Carry her off by force? Tell her that she was there to do his bidding?

Furiously recognising that at the moment she seemed to have the upper hand, he got out of the car, pulled her bag from the boot and handed it to her. She hadn't been joking—he had never seen a woman travel with such a small suitcase.

His eyes travelled to the pretty little shoes she wore—delicate, sexy little kitten heels, which showed the delectable curves of her tiny ankles. 'If you're planning to explore the city, then I suggest you wear something more sensible than those to walk in,' he said tightly. *'Fino ad allora, cara.'*

# CHAPTER NINE

ELLA glanced around her hotel accommodation with a combination of excitement and disbelief—because the 'room' she had imagined staying in was actually a suite—and nearly as big as the ground floor of her home in England!

She let her eyes drift over to the floor-to-ceiling windows, which commanded a breathtaking view of the sapphire sweep of the sea beyond. Tiny cotton wool clouds batted playfully at one another in the vast blue arena of the sky, and sunlight glinted off the sleek lines of distant yachts.

On the other side of the bay she could see hills clothed in dark green, with ice-white villas set like jewels within them. It was a combination of natural beauty and vast wealth—a world accessible only to the very few—and in any other circumstances she would be pinching herself and enjoying every second of it.

She ran her fingertips over the petal of a waxy orchid, telling herself that she would be crazy not to enjoy at least *some* of this once-in-a-lifetime experience.

She dressed for sightseeing, putting on a pair of flat strappy sandals that matched her ice-blue sun-dress, and tying her hair back in a blue ribbon. She finished off with a wide-brimmed straw hat, and as she checked herself in one of the mirrors she could see the image she presented was cool and contained. Good. Long may it last.

The day was bakingly hot, but a light breeze stopped it from being oppressive and the hat had been a good idea. Nico had been right about the walking bit, for the hilly streets around the harbour were all cobbled—picturesque, but hardgoing. She peered in all the shop windows, where stores selling luxury goods and clothes jostled next to those selling boat accessories. So far, all pretty predictable.

There were pavement cafés galore, and she found an empty seat and sat outside one, ordering an extremely expensive cup of coffee. She sat sipping cappuccino and watching the people come and go. The main cause of congestion really did seem to be centred around the art gallery dedicated to Juan Lopez. At one point two coaches disgorged their contents at the top of one of the quaint streets, and as they surged forward it felt a bit like being outside a football ground before the match started.

Ella got out her notebook and wrote for a little while, and then went off and found a bookshop.

Inside, it was dark and deliciously cool. There was a whole section about Juan Lopez, but Ella's attention was distracted by a part of the shop given over entirely to books about the ruling family of Mardivino.

Here there were biographies and picture books,

family portraits and single portraits. In a sweet little tome entitled *Just Like Us*, she found a photo of Nico as a baby—a chubby-faced little cherub, wearing a cascading lace christening robe, being cradled in the arms of his nurse. Maybe that was normal for Royal princes, but she happened to know that his mother had died when Nico was just a baby.

There was a whole muted and solemn chapter about the death of the young Queen, and a heartbreaking shot of the three boys—the two older boys clad in matching dark grey coats and a crying Nico being held by another nurse—as they watched the flower-decked coffin file past.

She had read about the death of his mother during her research, of course, but seeing it here—in black and white and in Mardivino itself—somehow made it more real and more poignant.

It made her see him as flesh and blood—someone who really *would* bleed if you cut him. It made him seem lovable and in need of love—but surely that was just wishful thinking on her part?

Her fingers twitched irresistibly onto a chapter devoted entirely to Nico, entitled 'The Daredevil Prince'. Here were snatched shots of Nico the action man among the formal poses—Nico sailing a yacht, giving a thumbs up at the top of a snowy mountain, and astride a monstrously large-looking motorbike.

Ella read on, engrossed, until she glanced at her watch and saw to her horror that she should have been back at L'Etoile ten minutes ago. But she couldn't get the image of the motherless baby out of her mind. Did his love for all things fast and dangerous stem from a childhood without the grounding of a mother, with palace servants forbidden by protocol to show him real love? Or was that too simplistic an explanation?

She sped towards the hotel to find him waiting for her, leaning against the door of his car and her heart turned over.

His posture was outwardly relaxed, but as she grew closer she could see the tell-tale look of irritation that hardened his autocratic features and made his black eyes glitter. Her tender concern vanished under that cold look of censure.

'Sorry I'm late,' she said automatically.

'Not very *professional* of you,' he bit out—because he had felt strangely out of place, hanging around the car like a chauffeur. 'Perhaps it pleases you to make me wait?' he mused. 'Did you do so deliberately?'

'Oh, for goodness' sake! Of course I didn't—I just lost track of the time.'

She was completely unapologetic! Quite the opposite, in fact! Nico was consumed by a simmering rage overpowered by a bubbling frustration. He looked down into her flushed face, at her parted lips, and felt the urge to kiss her as a kind of punishment—to tell her that no one *ever* kept him waiting.

He held the door of the car open, shaking his head slightly. A kiss? As a kind *punishment*? Who the hell did he think he was kidding?

As she moved towards the door he had opened for her, her bare arm brushed against his. It was the briefest and most fleeting contact, but it was like the sizzle of electricity, tingling fire over her skin, and she stepped back as if she had been stung.

'Don't,' she whispered.

Their eyes met.

'Don't what?' He could feel the tiny hairs standing up at the back of his neck and he stared back at her, angry and slightly appalled at himself for being so affected by such an innocent touch. 'What did I do, *cara*?' he mocked. 'Don't blame me for your own feelings. You want me. You still want me—you're just too hypocritical to admit it.'

He walked round to the driver's seat and slammed the door behind him, leaving Ella to shakily take her place beside him.

Ignore it, she told herself. Because if you don't you'll only have to admit he's right.

The car screeched away and Ella stole a glance at Nico's stony profile.

'Who's sulking now?' she questioned.

With an effort he roused himself out of his reverie. 'Not me.'

'Just don't want to talk?'

He smiled. 'Talk away.'

'Will you tell me a little bit about Mardivino, then?'

It was, he admitted grudgingly, exactly the right thing to say. It took his mind off the ache in his groin and the idea—almost unthinkable—that bedding Ella Scott once more was by no means certain.

'What do you wish to know?'

'Everything.'

'"Everything" is a tall order, *cara*,' he mused. But his eyes on the mountain road ahead of him, he started to tell her of Mardivino's history in a voice that grew unexpectedly dreamy, and then sometimes fiery as he recounted crusades and battles for the prized land. He talked of Spanish Conquistadors and Italian aristocrats and French counts, who had all fought for ownership over the centuries, until at last agreeing to share the spoils of the exquisite island, set like a jewel in the sea.

His passion was infectious, and Ella found herself listening with the rapt attention of a child being told a wonderful story—but it wasn't just the story that captured her imagination—it was him. You could watch a man closely when you were listening to him—could remind yourself of his passion and his strength and then wish you hadn't.

But if she pushed that kind of thought away then even more troubling memories hurtled in to replace them—with graphic recall. She could almost see the moist flick of his tongue against his lips, almost feel it on her belly, against her thighs…

But her whirling thoughts were stilled by the sight of what lay before her. She had been so caught up in them that she had taken little notice of the view whizzing by outside the limousine window. But now high, gilded gates were parting and Ella stared ahead, her breath catching in the back of her throat as they opened onto the Rainbow Palace.

Her first impression was that it looked like a stage-set. Something that was real and yet not quite real. She wondered if behind its glittering walls she would find an empty stage and pieces of wood propping it up? Just as she wondered what really lay beneath all the different masks that Nico wore. Was nothing real in his world?

From a distance the palace really *did* look like a rainbow, with the whole spectrum of vibrant, dazzling colours from violet right through to a rich and royal red. It was only as the car grew closer that Ella could make out the tiny mosaic pieces of stone. It was all an illusion, not substance. Not a rainbow at all.

But as she got out of the car Ella began to get some idea of the perspective of the place, and it was vast. Emerald squares of perfectly manicured grass were edged with velvety dark red roses. There was a formal fountain playing the music of scattering water, and a wonderful statue of a woman that looked so real that Ella felt like reaching out to test whether it was marble-cold or whether real blood coursed through the stone veins.

'Come,' said Nico, looking down at her.

'I'm slightly overwhelmed,' she said truthfully.

His hard mouth softened by a fraction. When she stopped fighting him, she was really very sweet. 'Well, don't be. It's just the place where I live.'

But how many people in the world lived in places like this one? It would always mark him out as different, because Nico *was* different. And it would be worthwhile to remember that.

He led her through seemingly endless corridors that were hung with enormous oil-paintings of men and women wearing lavish silk and lace gowns. Dark-haired, autocratic portraits, whose mesmeric and glittering black eyes marked them out as his ancestors.

It was a different world.

Eventually he pushed open a door and Ella found herself in an office—or at least a room that was doing a passable imitation of masquerading as an office—because offices did not usually contain antique desks, nor have drapes that glimmered to the floor in costly folds.

'You can work from here,' he said.

Work. Yes, of course.

It was difficult not to be dazzled. He looked so at home in these lavish surroundings—but of course he would—it was his home, for heaven's sake! But it had the effect of making Nico of the beach hut and Nico the lover seem like mere figments of her imagination.

'Okay,' she said, and gave a brisk smile. 'Can you organise a map of the island for me?'

'There's one here.' He leaned over the desk and Ella caught the faint drift of a musky lemon fragrance. She briefly closed her eyes in despair. Scent was so evocative—it took you to places you would rather not go—and she had headily breathed in that scent when her face had been nuzzled into the warmth of his sleeping neck.

'Will this do?' He opened a large book showing a brightly coloured map of Mardivino.

She moved beside him and looked over his shoulder, and he turned his head and their eyes held. She found herself yielding, helpless in the soft, dark light that blazed over her.

'Gabriella,' he murmured caressingly.

She shook her head desperately, like a woman who was trying to convince herself. 'No.'

'Your lips tell me one thing while your eyes are saying something very different,' he observed quietly.

He lifted the tips of her fingers and touched them to his lips, feeling them tremble at that one brief contact. He increased the pressure of his mouth and saw her eyelids flutter to a close.

'Nico,' she whispered.

They fluttered open again and her eyes were like pure gleaming emeralds amid the tangle of dark lashes. He gave a small groan, briefly tangling his hands into the tawny splendour of her hair before pulling her into his arms, the dark light of conquest firing his eyes as he stared down at her.

'Nico, what?' he demanded huskily.

'This is...*wrong*,' she breathed.

But she made no move to stop him, to push him away or to detach herself from his embrace, and all he could do was drink in these lips and this face, which had haunted his dreams since that all-too-brief encounter of such tender and sensual beauty. And then he could wait no longer—could think no further than the need to taste and to kiss her once more.

Her hands caught and gripped his broad shoulders as if they were magnetised, her breath escaping in a gasp that mingled with his breath as she felt the hard, seeking warmth of his mouth.

'Oh,' she moaned weakly against him, as his hands splayed down to cup her buttocks, bringing her closer into the hard cradle of his desire. 'Oh!'

Urgently, he moved his hand downwards and drifted his fingers up her bare thigh, scraping the tips in soft, enticing circles. He felt her legs part in invitation.

He felt as if he was going to explode. As if he wanted to rip the cheap little dress from her and take her right there. He moved her panties aside and delved into her hot, sticky heat, and she gasped with pleasure.

'I want you, Gabriella,' he ground out. 'I want you so much.'

And she wanted him, too. So badly. Boldly she touched him back, drifting her hand over his hardness to feel it increase, and he tore his mouth away from hers.

'Come with me to my apartment,' he said urgently. 'Let me make love to you all the rest of the day and all through the night, until you have emptied me of all my seed.'

It was a curiously powerful and unexpected thing to say, and it shook Ella even more than the light, expert caress of his fingers and the memory of his passionate kiss. Quite what she would have done next, she didn't know—and she never had the chance to find out because there was a loud peremptory rap on the door and Nico froze.

She looked at him in horror. 'The door!' she whispered.

He acted instinctively, tugging her dress down into place and moving away from her, raking his hand back through his ruffled dark hair, aware that her musky perfume was still lingering on his fingers. He let out a brief, shuddering sigh.

'Yes?' he shot out.

The door opened and a man stood there, and even if she hadn't studied photos of him earlier that day Ella would have known instantly that it was Nico's eldest brother Gianferro.

She tried to picture the scene through his eyes. Outwardly, they were both decent—no clothing in disarray—but it must be obvious just what had been about to happen. Their heightened colour and hectic eyes held a sexual tension so taut that it felt as if it might snap, as if a mere breath could shatter it—and Gianferro just had. She wished that the floor would open up and swallow her as the Crown Prince stared at her.

Gianferro's dark, unreadable eyes moved from her

to Nico. 'Forgive me,' he said icily. 'This is obviously an inopportune moment.'

His expression was one that Nico could read perfectly, but he met the disapproving accusation head-on, brazening it out. And why the hell shouldn't he? He was not a child, and his brother was not his keeper! If he barged in on two consenting adults, then he just might not like what he would find.

'Gianferro,' he said, as coolly as if he had been taking tea with a woman on some sun-dappled terrace. 'I would like you to meet Ella Scott, who will be using her travel expertise to advise us. Ella, this is my brother, the Crown Prince Gianferro.'

Briefly and autocratically Gianferro inclined his head, and Ella sent Nico an agonised glance. Was she supposed to curtsey, or what? In silent understanding he sent her a barely perceptible shake of the head.

'And what is your *particular* area of expertise, Miss Scott?' drawled the heir.

She knew what he was implying, and if only she had been a sheet of paper she would have crumpled into a ball of shame. But adaptability was the name of the game. She couldn't pretend that what had just happened *hadn't* happened, but she could deal with it. She had committed no crime and she was not his cringeing subject.

'Actually, I specialise in the small-is-beautiful market, Your Royal Highness,' she said smoothly. 'Which sort of sums Mardivino up, don't you think?'

Nico sent her a silent look of admiration. Most

women of his acquaintance would have blushed and stammered their way out of *that* one. He had been about to leap in to protect Ella from Gianferro's barely veiled hostility, but now he could see that she was perfectly capable of looking after herself.

'Nico hasn't told me how long you intend staying,' said the Crown Prince.

'That's because I haven't yet decided how long I need to. I haven't signed any kind of contract.' She couldn't miss the unmistakable look of surprise on his face. And on Nico's. Presumably they were used to making the decisions, not employing people who made their own! 'But you can rest assured that my work will be accomplished in as short a time as possible,' she continued sweetly, seeing Nico's eyes narrow into dark, glittering shards. He wants to call all the shots, she recognised. And I am not going to let him.

'I am very pleased to hear it,' said Gianferro. He shot Nico another unfathomable look. 'Perhaps I could see you alone for a moment, Nicolo?'

Nico raised his eyebrows. 'As you can see, I'm a little busy.'

Ella felt her cheeks flaming. Was Gianferro trying to get Nico out of the office to warn him not to make love to her? Well, he could save his breath!

She closed the open book on the desk and picked it up, somehow managing a cool and professional smile. 'I was actually just about to leave,' she said. 'My trip here today was only intended to be an introductory one, and in future I will be working on my own.' Her green eyes flashed Nico a warning. 'I certainly won't need to waste any more of Nico's time.'

Nico's mouth tightened. She was playing him like a virtuoso, knowing that he would be unable to object in his brother's presence. How dared she? 'Will there be anything else, Gianferro?'

'I'll see you at dinner.'

Nico shook his head. 'I don't think you will.'

There was a pause while the brothers' eyes met and engaged in a silent ebony duel. 'Then perhaps you could make me an appointment in your diary some time this year?' returned Gianferro sardonically, and left the room with a curt nod.

Once he had gone, and the door was closed behind him, Ella rounded on Nico, her voice beginning to tremble with rage. 'How *dare* you expose me to that kind of humiliation?' she accused.

'I certainly wasn't expecting my brother to walk in,' he said drily.

'No?'

'Of course not. I would have gone to the precaution of locking the door had that been the case.'

Ella could have screamed! He didn't look in the least bit repentant—on the contrary, he simply looked irritated, as if he had had his fun cut short. Which, when she stopped to think about it, he had. 'Did you think you could just come up here and have your wicked way with me? Is that what you thought?' she demanded. 'Your *droit de seigneur*?'

'I wasn't doing much thinking,' he drawled. 'And I hadn't planned it, no, if that's what you want to know.' His eyes glittered. 'You are just too damned irresistible, *cara*.'

'What kind of a tramp must I have looked to your brother?'

'Tramp?' He raised his brows in surprise. 'That's fairly emotive language, Ella. My brother is no innocent—he won't judge you, or me, for doing what comes so naturally to a man and a woman. I really should have locked the door...' he said, half to himself.

That just about did it. 'I don't care about him judging me!' declared Ella, wildly contradicting herself in the heat of the moment. 'I'm judging myself, if you must know—and I'm pretty appalled at my own behaviour!'

'Why?'

'Because it was wrong—you know it was wrong!'

'I disagree.' He regarded her steadily, wondering if she had any idea just how magnificent she looked when she was angry. 'You want me, Gabriella,' he observed coolly. 'Don't deny it. You know you do.'

She stared at him, at the hot, glittering eyes and the autocratic curve of his sensual lips, and her heart flipped and there was nothing she could do to stop it. 'Oh, I don't deny that on some fundamental level I do—sure I do. But that's not how I operate, Nico—women rarely do. There has to be more than pure physical attraction.'

'That didn't seem to bother you last time,' he commented insultingly.

'That's because—' She bit her lip, terrified of showing her vulnerability, of letting him know that she had been beginning to build all kinds of dreams about him. She had seen him for what she had believed him to be—her strong, powerful rescuer and an intelligent, provocative man. But that had been an illusion that had crumbled into dust.

'Because?' he prompted arrogantly.

'Maybe I did behave hot-headedly,' she admitted. 'But I thought that you...' She cleared her throat. 'At the time I didn't realise that you...'

'Were a prince?' he supplied drily. 'Well, now you do, and I must say it's the first time that it's ever worked against me.'

Her eyes flashed fire. 'It's more than that, and you know it!'

'What is it?' he grated. 'Explain it to me! Why are you so hung up on my title, Gabriella?'

'It's not the *title*—'

'Isn't it?' he challenged.

'No! It's the fact that you didn't tell me! I don't like dishonesty in a man.'

'There is rarely total truth between new lovers,' he bit out frustratedly.

Maybe he was right. But it was suddenly about more than that. He's never failed before, Ella realised. This is possibly the first time in his life he hasn't got what he wanted—at least with a woman.

For a moment she felt filled with a heady sense of

power, but that soon fled and was replaced by something much more satisfactory. Because right then, despite everything, Ella felt his *equal*.

She gave him a thin smile. 'And now, if you don't mind, I really do want to go back to the hotel and make some notes.'

He could see that he was going to make no further headway. At least, not right now. But there would be plenty more opportunities. 'Okay,' he agreed easily. 'Let's go. We can continue this fascinating discussion later, over dinner.'

'No, we can not,' she refuted, revelling even more in his look of surprise. But she needed to safeguard herself—not just against his sexual charisma but against her own helpless reaction to it—and to do that she needed to put distance between them. 'I am going to spend the evening in my beautiful and lavish suite, and I shall order something up from Room Service.'

She saw his lips part in amazement as she walked past him, her head held high, and flung the door open—though more as a protective device than anything else. The room was now on view to the whole corridor, and with servants and brothers potentially lingering in the background surely he wouldn't dare try anything else?

By now he was laughing softly at her extravagant behaviour. 'Oh, but your surrender will be sweetness itself, *cara*.'

'It isn't going to happen, Nico,' she replied tartly, and hoped that her words carried more conviction than she felt.

# CHAPTER TEN

AFTER a long and luxurious bath, and a delicious supper that she ate on her terrace overlooking the harbour, Ella began to pore over the map Nico had given her. By the time she fell into bed she was exhausted.

But fatigue did nothing to block out the images of his black mocking eyes, and when eventually she fell asleep it was to dream of Nico.

A car picked her up the following morning, and drove her to the palace, and a servant took her to the office that Nico had shown her the day before. There was a small cut-glass bowl of scented white roses sitting on the desk, with an envelope beside it, which she ripped open.

Inside was a note from Nico. It was the first time she had seen his handwriting and it was rather like the man himself—uncompromising and bold.

It said: *Today I have taken my bike up into the mountains. Will you have dinner with me tonight?* And it was signed simply, *Nico*.

She sat back in her chair and looked out of the window onto the palace courtyard. Should she?

Well, what else was she going to do? Sit in her suite night after night, ordering up Room Service? She picked up her pen and began to make notes.

It didn't take her long to discover that an office was an office wherever it was—palace or not. The only real difference about this one was that it was so *quiet*. She hadn't always worked from home, she had done her share in other places, where there had always been a buzz, with people stopping by for coffee, or the sound of telephones ringing and fax machines disgorging their pages. But here the silence was uncanny. Did the servants move around on noiseless feet? Probably. It hit her in a sudden rush of understanding just how *lonely* it would be, to be a Royal.

She worked hard, marking out places she wanted to visit, and she was just wondering what to do about lunch—she didn't imagine that there was a vending machine sitting outside the throne room!—when there was a rap at the door.

'Come in,' she called, and the door opened to reveal the tall, imposing figure of Prince Gianferro.

Somehow she wasn't a bit surprised.

She rose to her feet. 'I honestly don't know whether or not I'm supposed to curtsey,' she admitted.

He nodded. 'I think you can be excused,' he observed drily. 'This is, after all, a rather informal meeting. I wondered—since I believe you have been working all morning—whether you would care to see the palace gardens? After that, I could arrange to have some lunch sent here.'

So he wasn't actually inviting her for lunch! *He*

*wants to suss me out,* she thought suddenly. She nodded. 'I should like that very much.'

'Come.'

It was a quiet and silky command, but she thought it came to him as naturally as breathing—which, when she came to think about it, it probably did. He would have been obeyed without question since he was barely out of the cradle—how must that affect a man's character development? she wondered. How had it affected Nico's?

As they emerged from the cool marble corridor into the bright sunlit gardens, she felt a ripple of sensation whispering over her skin at the thought of Gianferro's youngest brother. She wished he were with her. He would protect her from his brother, she realised, from the searching questions she was certain would follow. Or maybe Gianferro was too subtle to interrogate her outright? Would not a man of his birthright establish and direct matters in a far more understated way?

He paused beside a circular bed of the most heavenly roses Ella had ever seen—great rumpled globes of saffron, the petal-tips edged in apricot-pink—and the sweet scent of the massed flowers wafted up to her. She breathed it in.

'Your work is going well?' Gianferro asked casually.

Ella nodded. 'I can see a lot that could be done.'

'Really?' Dark eyebrows were raised in imperious question.

It was Nico who was in charge of touristic development on the island, and Nico who had brought her here. She was not going to brief his curious brother before she had even decided herself just what plans could be implemented.

'Yes, really,' she echoed softly, and saw his mouth harden. She had not intended to be rude. She drew in a deep breath and looked around. 'These really are the most exquisite flowers I have ever seen,' she said quietly. 'And such an unusual planting.'

There was a pause while she saw his eyes narrow, and then he nodded, as if he had just learned something, but she couldn't miss the sudden bleakness that flared at the back of the black eyes that were so like Nico's.

'They are roses named after my mother. My father had them planted after her death,' he said flatly. 'If you look closely you will see that the bushes form the initials of her name.'

'I'm sorry. I didn't mean—'

'No.' He shook his head. 'It was a thoughtful and intelligent observation.'

Ella was too flustered to feel patronized—and besides, she did not think that had been his intention.

'Perhaps,' he continued thoughtfully, 'since you wield much influence over my brother, you could persuade him to stop tearing around and putting his life at risk? And while you are about it a word or two about mountain climbing might prove useful.'

Ella stared at him. She had no experience of this kind of life, and yet instinct told her that this was not a commonplace conversation for the heir to the throne to be having.

'I have no influence over Nico,' she said.

'Oh, I disagree. You have enough for him to bring you—an outsider—here to work for him.'

'That doesn't happen often?'

'No,' he said emphatically.

'Why don't you tell him your concerns yourself?'

'You think I have not done so?' He gave an odd kind of smile. 'Life may move on, but relationships with siblings stay firmly rooted in the past—and so it is with my brothers. Our battles mimic those of our palace nursery! But a man who courts danger will achieve no lasting happiness. In any sphere of his life. Danger is both seductive and addictive, but Nicolo's life is mapped out in a way that other men's are not. His destiny is written, his path clearly defined. In all directions.'

He was warning her, Ella realised. *Warning her off!* Suddenly she felt an overwhelming urge to kick against this rigidity and restraint. No wonder Nico courted danger—if his life was to be a straitjacket!

She stared up at Gianferro with clear green eyes. 'I really ought to be getting back to work,' she said apologetically. 'I have a lot to get through, and Nico is taking me out for dinner.'

She hid a small, determined smile. Suddenly she found she was looking forward to it!

\*    \*    \*

Nico was just about to ring her when his mobile thrilled into life. His eyes widened fractionally when he saw the number flash up, and his lips curved into a smile.

'Nico?'

'Gabriella,' he murmured. 'I can't quite believe it. The woman who behaved in such a cavalier fashion when I gave her my number is actually using it! What kind of day have you had?'

'Productive.' And interesting. 'Are you still free tonight?'

He felt the automatic quickening of his pulse. 'What time did you have in mind?' he said softly.

'I meant for dinner,' she said immediately.

'Why, so did I,' he returned, his voice mocking her with innocent reprimand. 'What did you think I meant?'

'Nothing.'

He smiled. He rather liked her chastened. 'I'll pick you up.'

'Okay. About eight? Oh, and Nico?'

'Mmm?'

'Do you drive your motorbike very fast?'

He frowned. 'That's the whole point of having one, Gabriella. I'll see you later.' And he hung up.

She opened up the wardrobe, trying to be enthusiastic, but it wasn't easy. It was all very well, defiantly bringing only the barest minimum of clothes here, but she was going to have to wear some things twice if she stayed beyond a week. And he had already seen her in the black dress!

She stood beneath the jets of the power shower. Not that she would need to stay beyond that, she told herself firmly. She had conceived a simple idea to put to Nico, which she was certain would work—and then she could go. Before she did something really stupid, like starting to care for him.

But you *do* care for him, mocked an inner voice.

She switched the shower off with a flourish, and wrapped herself in a fluffy white robe.

She did *not* care for him. She was attracted to him sexually, that was all.

But you don't *do* sex on its own, Ella, taunted that infuriating voice again. You know you don't. And you've never done sex like *that* before.

She had a white broderie anglaise dress that she had been saving—though she wasn't quite sure what she had been saving it for. So after much deliberation, she put it on. It was sweet and feminine, with tiny cap sleeves that she could just about get away with. She was tempted to plait her hair, but in the end she decided against it and wore it loose—she didn't want to look as though she was auditioning for a part in *The Sound of Music*!

She was ten minutes late, and he was waiting for her downstairs, seated casually on a plush leather sofa. A man with a suspiciously bulky jacket was positioned conspicuously close by. As the lift doors opened the normal chatter of the foyer died to a hush and Nico rose to his feet.

People were watching him—either openly or not

quite so openly. Women, some standing with their husbands, positioned themselves so that they could be seen at their most flattering angle—pushing their breasts out and sucking in their already concave stomachs. But he was not looking at the women.

He was looking at her.

She saw him give a brief, barely discernible nod to the man, and was vaguely aware that faces were now turning in *her* direction, their expressions slightly incredulous. And she realised how cheap her dress must look in comparison to their designer finery.

What happened next was like some smooth, well-practised machine whirring into action. Subtle signals must have been given, for a pathway was magically formed, leaving their exit clear just as a long, low car purred to the front of the building, with a chauffeur behind the wheel.

She realised that she had never met him anywhere quite so public before—*that* would explain the high-profile security.

'Is it always like this?' Ella asked, as she wriggled onto the back seat and the door was slammed shut on them.

He turned to her, thinking how shining and fresh she looked in her simple white dress. 'Like what?'

She shrugged her shoulders. 'So choreographed. As if everything has been planned right down to the last second.'

'Not quite the last second,' he commented wryly. 'Since you were late.'

'Sorry.'

'It's okay.' He smiled.

'Do you like it—all the fuss?'

'It's just the way it is. What I cannot change I have to accept—or my life would be intolerable. I escape it whenever I can.'

'Like on the motorbike?'

'The motorbike, yes—you seem to be obsessed with my damned motorbike! And, yes, before you ask—the jet-ski, too! You know what they say—big toys for big boys.' His eyes glittered as he saw the faint rush of colour to her cheeks. 'Now, stop asking me so many questions and tell me how you got on today.'

'Not bad. I've got a few ideas.'

'Such as?'

She gave him a rather prim smile. 'I'm not going to talk about it until I've worked it out properly. But I've made a list of all the places on the island I'd like to visit.'

Which sounded a little like a refusal to tell him!

'Right,' he said, in a rather dazed voice. 'We're here.'

The restaurant had clearly been chosen as much for its discreet setting as its breathtaking view of the sea, but it only reinforced Ella's sensation of inhabiting a different world. There were women wearing a fortune in gems glittering around their necks, and she spotted a famous actress getting very cosy with a man who was definitely not her husband.

But all eyes were on them, watching as they weaved their way to a table in a candlelit alcove.

He ordered red wine, and then a steaming dish that arrived in a covered and distinctively patterned deep blue earthenware pot.

'What a beautiful dish,' observed Ella.

'You like it? It is produced only in Islaroca, on the north west corner of the island.'

'I've never seen anything like it before.'

'You soon will—there's a big export drive going on at the moment.'

It had been Nico's baby—his attempt to change something of the island's reputation for being just a tax haven for people with too much money. On an island with few natural resources, it seemed madness not to capitalise on the pottery industry—though Gianferro had initially opposed the expansion. His damned brother and his need to control!

When the waitress took the lid off the casserole, Ella stilled for a moment and turned her eyes towards Nico. 'I recognise this,' she said, sniffing.

He held her gaze. 'That's because I cooked it for you at the beach,' he said softly. 'Our national dish.' The corners of his mouth lifted in a sardonic smile. 'But this one probably won't be quite as good as mine.'

He was right, it wasn't—but Ella suspected that was because her hunger was not so honed as it had been back then.

And senses were both evocative and nostalgic—

taste no less so than sight or sound. One mouthful was enough to transport her back to that time and place, to recall his kindness and his gentleness towards her. Her memory froze and then galloped forward, to rekindle even more evocative memories...

She gazed across the table towards him and felt the tiptoe of longing take slow, skittering steps up her spine.

He saw the tip of her tongue flick out to moisten her lips and felt the dry, hard ache of need as he watched her.

'Gabriella—' he whispered.

But his words were interrupted by a small flurry of activity at the door. Heads were raised and turned in its direction, and Nico's eyes narrowed as a flamboyant-looking man with a shock of yellow hair beamed and began to walk towards their table.

He gave a small sigh, but Ella heard it. It was tinged with resignation and irritation, but his dark, handsome face did not make a flicker of reaction.

'Who is it?'

'It's the owner and sometimes chef,' he answered. 'He's a bit of a star on the island, as modern-day chefs so often are.' He gave a cynical smile. 'I thought he was in Paris.'

Ella stared at him as realisation began to dawn. 'Has he...?' She hesitated, because her supposition sounded so bizarre. 'He hasn't flown back all the way from Paris especially because you happen to be having dinner in his restaurant?'

His eyes mocked her. 'Well, what do you think?'

She thought it was completely crazy, that was what she thought.

Ella watched while the owner bowed to Nico, his eyes barely giving her a second glance. As though she didn't count. But, oh, Nico counted—that much was plain to see from the fawning bonhomie, the implication that Nico could demand a fresh strawberry flown from the Highlands of Scotland and a minion would immediately be dispatched to secure it.

After he had left, Nico studied her. 'Do you understand a little now, Gabriella—why I did not tell you who I was?'

And Ella nodded, feeling…feeling as if she had somehow been too hard on him. Had she been guilty of looking at it from just *her* viewpoint, without thinking of his?

'It must have been quite something…to be anonymous,' she said slowly.

'It was a taste of freedom which I found exhilarating.' He shrugged. 'And one which was heady enough to allow me to repress the knowledge that I was keeping something back.'

The same sense of freedom that made people such fans of dangerous sports, she realised. It all made sense now. 'I wouldn't have reacted quite so angrily,' she said, 'if I'd known.'

A faint smile touched his lips. 'No, I'm sure you wouldn't. But in one way I'm glad you didn't know. For once it was good to have someone behave…' He shrugged his shoulders and gave a faint smile. 'Well, *normally*, I guess.' And that had not changed. He could never remember having such a candid conversation with a woman.

Her heart was thudding, her palms grown clammy with this new turn of developments. And he was doing it again—appealing to some soft inner core of her. But surely that would only complicate things.

Because what he said didn't actually *change* anything. It made his actions more understandable, but his motivation remained the same. He had wanted sex with her, and that was what had happened. It might have been the most wonderful thing in her life so far, but she imagined that it was like that all the time for a man like Nico.

And the most fundamental fact of all could not be changed.

That he was a prince and she was just an ordinary young woman from the countryside. And unless she kept that to the forefront of her mind she was heading straight for heartbreak.

Nico drifted his eyes over her. She had drunk, he noted, very little—was that deliberate?—but she seemed less defensive than before. Nonetheless, instinct still told him that he must tread very carefully. He sensed that she was close to surrender, but one false move and he could blow it.

Later, when they were seated in the intimate interior of the luxury car, Ella waited breathlessly for a move that did not come. She was aware that her overriding feeling was one of disappointment. Stop it, she thought. Stop wishing for something that could only ever be bittersweet.

The car pulled up outside L'Etoile and he turned to her, his dark eyes glittering. 'Shall we drive to some of the towns and villages on your list tomorrow?' he suggested.

Ella nodded, her heart beating so hard that she was surprised he couldn't hear it. 'Okay.'

'We'll make a day of it,' he said casually. 'And I'll bring a picnic.'

# CHAPTER ELEVEN

'YOU know that Gianferro spoke to me yesterday?'

'Did he?' Nico didn't take his eyes off the road. They were heading towards one of Mardivino's least pretty villages because Gabriella wanted to have a look at it, but she hadn't told him why.

'I'm thinking,' she had said, and would not be swayed.

It was, he thought wryly, an oddly erotic experience to tussle with a woman who would not be swayed.

'So what did he say?' he questioned, as he negotiated a narrow road that was a dream on the bike but not quite so amenable to the four-wheel drive he had considered necessary for this journey.

'He worries about you.'

Nico gave a short laugh. 'Don't tell me—he gave you the "dangerous sports" lecture?'

'You know about that?'

'Of course.' He changed down a gear. 'It wouldn't matter if I was strolling sedately along the beach at Solajoya—if Gianferro didn't approve, he would attempt to talk me out of it. It's less a fear of the consequences, in his case, and more the fact that he likes to control—it's in his blood. He takes his heir-to-the-

throne responsibilities a touch too seriously sometimes. That's why Guido doesn't live here any more.
Why he got out just as soon as he could.'

'You don't mind?'

'Oh, I've just learned to ignore him,' he said softly.

'Sounds like a bit of a communication problem to
me.'

'Skip the amateur psychology, Gabriella. If I want
advice about how to deal with my brother, then I'll
ask for it.'

There was silence in the car, the kind of claustro-
phobic, in-car silence that grew like a heavy, oppressive cloud.

'That was harsh of me,' said Nico eventually.

'No, you're right.' She shrugged. 'Your relationship with your brother is none of my business.'

No, it wasn't. Her personal opinion wasn't the reason he had brought her here—her professional opinion, maybe. But that wasn't strictly true, either, was
it? The job had simply been a manoeuvre to get her
here; her seduction had been uppermost in his mind.
But she had embraced the project with an enthusiasm
that impressed him, and yet he still remained a
stranger to her bed.

His brow creased into a frown. Nothing was turning
out as he had planned. Why was she continuing to
hold him at arm's length when he knew damned well
that she wanted him?

'We're here,' he bit out, as the car bumped its way
over the dusty road that led to the village.

It was an unprepossessing place—high and barren, the sea so far away that it looked like a sapphire strip of ribbon in the distance. Nico looked around him; he hadn't been here for years.

The local people still harvested their olive crop, but these days they had to compete with the mass-farming methods of larger countries, such as Greece, and it showed. The place looked run-down, the small restaurant on the main street tired. They walked through the village and back, struck by its emptiness and its silence. No one was on the streets bar a couple of children scratching symbols in the dust, who stared at them with wide, curious eyes. Certainly no one recognised him. It was like a ghost town, thought Nico dazedly.

'No one ever comes here,' he said slowly, as their footsteps drew them back to the car. Not even him. He might tear around the island on his motorbike, but he never really stopped long enough to look. To stand and stare. He shook his head, like a man waking from a long sleep. What could he do to help these people? he wondered.

You didn't have to be the heir to care, he realized, and part of him resented the fact that it had taken this stranger, this *Englishwoman*, to show him this. But who else would have dared? Who would have looked him straight in the eyes and said the things to him that Gabriella had done?

And didn't her complete lack of connection with

his island give him the rare opportunity to express himself? What would it matter to her?

'I have neglected places such as this.'

She heard the guilt in his voice. 'You can't do everything, Nico,' she said softly.

'I could do more,' he said suddenly.

'I agree. In fact, I think I have a solution for places like this—well, certainly this place in particular.'

She was good at her job, he recognised suddenly. Very good. His instinct that fresh eyes would provide a fresh perspective had been a sound one. Just so long as she understood her limitations...

Her hair looked like spun gold as the sun beat down on them, warming his skin, inexorably filling him with a languid feeling of contentment. She had sensibly worn a hat to shade her face, and it had the effect of making her look very pure and innocent.

Innocent?

With breathtaking clarity he recalled her skill as a lover, and the deep aching that he had been doing his best to suppress suddenly burst into life and dominated everything.

'Do you...do you want to hear it?' asked Ella, suddenly breathless—because when he looked at her like that it made her feel... She swallowed, suddenly aware of the sound of a distant bird, of the strong, heavy beat of her heart.

'Do I want to hear...what?' he questioned evenly, deliberately misunderstanding, deliberately sending her a silent, sensual message with his eyes.

She wanted him to stop that—and yet she wanted him to go on looking at her like that for ever. 'My...idea, of course.'

He gave a slow smile. 'Want to tell me about it over lunch?'

Her heart was now crashing a symphony beneath her breast. 'It's a little early for lunch.'

'We can look at the scenery for a while.'

Ella shrugged—as if it didn't matter, as if she didn't care. 'Okay,' she agreed, and wondered where the brisk, cool businesswoman had disappeared to. Lost in the soft ebony promise of his eyes, that was where.

He drove towards the interior, stopping the car near a small copse of trees she didn't recognise—tall, graceful trees, with broad leaves providing a canopy and tiny blue flowers intertwined. It was beautiful but it was secluded, Ella realised, her heart beating even faster. *So ask him to take you somewhere else,* mocked the inner voice of sense.

'Do you want to spread the rug out?' he asked carelessly. 'And I'll bring the picnic.'

Shutting the door on sense, she did as he asked, spreading the cashmere rug out on the grass with fingers that were trembling. As he put the basket down and sat beside her she knew what was about to happen. She wondered not would she be able to resist—but whether she really *wanted* to resist.

Nico leaned back on his elbows and studied her. Her body looked taut, expectant—oh, God, yes. It was shady beneath the trees and the dappled sunlight rippled over them in a kaleidoscope of gold.

'Why don't you take your hat off?' he suggested softly. 'I can't see your eyes.'

She wasn't sure she wanted him to. Wouldn't he be able to read in them her doubts, her fears? And, most of all, her longing. They were supposed to be working, yet working was the furthest thing on her mind right now.

But she removed it anyway, feeling as shy as if he had asked her to strip for him, and her hair tumbled down over her shoulders like heavy silk.

'Your beautiful eyes,' he murmured. 'So very green.'

His voice had dipped and softened, but his own eyes were bright—and hard. Her mouth felt dry and the tip of her tongue snaked out to moisten it. Say something, she thought. But words suddenly seemed as foreign as the place in which she found herself.

'Are you thirsty, *cara mia*?' he questioned, and his voice sounded husky and slumberous.

Italian, he had said, was the language of love. But this isn't love, she tried to tell herself. It's sex, pure and simple—for him.

'Stop it,' she whispered.

'Stop what?' he questioned, as he began to open the hamper. 'What kind of a host would I be if I didn't look after my guest?'

He had thought of bringing champagne, but champagne was too clichéd—and it held bitter memories.

She had offered him champagne as an empty gesture once before, but she had been angry with him then. She didn't look in the least bit angry now. She looked soft, and vulnerable, but ready and waiting—like a delicious cake just waiting to be cut. He took a silver flask from the hamper, filled a cup to the brim with iced lemon and handed it to her.

But Ella was shaking as she took it from him, her fingers trembling in a way over which she seemed to have no control. Some of the cool, delicious drink reached her mouth, but more of it splattered down the front of her dress, leaving damp splotches over the hectic rise and fall of her breasts like giant tears.

He took the cup from her with a hand so steady it could have performed brain surgery, and drank some himself. Then he put the cup down and leaned his face close to hers.

It swam in and out of focus—the dazzle of his eyes, the silken olive skin, the lush, sensual lines of his lips. She seemed to be able to breathe in his virile scent, and she was aware of the silence that surrounded them. The slow, heavy pounding of her heart was the only sound she could hear.

Yet *he* seemed so utterly in control—while inside she felt as fluttery as a captured butterfly. The balance is all wrong, she told herself, and yet deep down she knew that this was what she had wanted all the time.

'Gabriella,' he whispered. 'You have made me wait, and I can wait no longer.'

His breathtaking honesty made her melt—or maybe

it was the warmth of his breath on her skin that did that. Sometimes you could block out a need and a desire so much that when you gave it a peep of life it erupted and became unstoppable.

'We shouldn't be doing this,' she said helplessly, as he ran the flat of his hand down over her hair.

'Oh, yes, we should,' he murmured. 'It has been too long—much, much too long.'

'Nico—'

He stilled her words with the touch of his mouth, brushing his lips against hers with a light, experimental touch, feeling her shiver in response and then make a little moan of protest when he moved away again. He bit back a small smile of triumph as he kissed her again—only this time his hands slid up her back and captured her, moving her body hard against his.

Ella was lost in the piercing sweetness of him as he kissed her over and over again, until she was helpless with wanting. Deep, hard kisses, that sent her senses reeling as she moved restlessly beneath him, forgetting everything. Forgetting the deceit and the differences and all that had gone before, just kissing him, and touching him, the man whose own desire was like touch-paper to her senses.

He felt as if he was drowning, sucked deep and then deeper still into a dark swirling vortex of desire as he pulled her to the ground, overwhelmed by the need to take her. Swiftly.

'Nico!' His hand was on her leg, rucking her skirt up.

'Touch me,' he urged, hot fingertips finding the cool skin of her thigh. She gasped against his neck. 'Touch me.'

She moved her hand down, laying her palm over him to cup his hardness, and he moaned softly, almost helplessly. She felt a heady power because he was as much at her mercy as she was at his. She put her mouth close to his ear. 'You've...you've got me so I can't think straight...'

'Then don't think. Just enjoy it.' Like I do. He shuddered as her fingertips touched him so intimately. 'Oh, *Dio*, yes!' The words were torn from his lips in a warm torrent. All restraint had vanished. He had never felt so out of control—and it terrified him nearly as much as he exulted in the feeling. It was like standing on the edge of a cliff, knowing that you were going to jump even though to do so would be madness.

Aware that this was something he had to do, if it wasn't going to be over before it started, he pulled her hand away, taking it to his mouth and gently biting her fingers. '*Lentamente*. Take...it...slow...' he urged.

But he wasn't following his own advice, thought Ella, her head falling back against the rug as he began to slide her panties down over her knees. She felt the cool rush of air on her heated flesh and opened her mouth to protest that maybe they should move from here. That he was a prince…that this was all happening too quickly. But she opened her thighs, too…

And then his lips were on hers once more, and his fingers were delving into her honeyed warmth, and she was lost in the rhythm of a dance more ancient than either crown or privilege. And then she stopped thinking about that, and thought of Nico instead—this dazzling-eyed man who had haunted her thoughts and her dreams since the moment she had first laid eyes on him—touching her with such sweet accuracy so that she cried in ecstatic wonder against his skin.

Her mouth moved against the graze of his shadowed jaw, and she burrowed beneath his silk shirt to find skin even more silken where it stretched over hard muscle and sinew. She began to tug impatiently at his belt, and heard him give a low laugh of delight.

He stilled her hand as he lifted his head, and his ebony eyes were glazed with a desire that made them smoulder down at her like burning coal. He shook his head. 'No, let me,' he said roughly, his gaze never leaving her face as he unzipped his jeans.

He pushed her dress right up and moaned softly to discover that she was bra-less. He dipped his head to suck tightly on her nipple as he wriggled his jeans off, not wanting—not able—to wait to undress her completely. The little cries she was making were inciting him even more as he scrambled like a schoolboy to protect himself, and then there was no more waiting, and he plunged deep, deep inside her slick heat.

'Nico!' she gasped as he began to move, because last time it had not felt so full, or so tight, or so unutterably right. She threaded her fingers into his thick dark hair and pulled his head towards her, opening her mouth beneath his as if she couldn't get enough of him.

And Nico was lost…lost in something that was like new territory to him. He had always been a master of self-control, and usually he had the ability to take himself outside the act. To observe the woman and to lead—taking them both at the pace he wished them to follow, almost like a conductor of an orchestra.

But this time it was different. Was that because she had kept him on tenterhooks for what seemed like an eternity? Because he had never been quite sure whether this would actually happen, and, now that it was, its potent sweetness surpassed all his hot and wildest fantasies?

He found himself lost in a deep, dark pleasure where self was obliterated by sensation. His body no longer felt like his, but hers did. All his. His hands moved from her breasts to her hips, holding her tighter as he moved inside her over and over again. He felt that he might die if it did not end soon, yet he wanted it to last for ever.

Her cry split the air, her limbs tensed and then flailed, her eyes closing, her lips whispering his name like a prayer. And Nico followed her, dissolving into something so sweet that it felt sinful.

For a moment he felt the same heady sense of triumph he always experienced when he broke in a new and difficult stallion, or when he sailed hard against the wind.

And then the feeling was gone, and he was left with the more familiar feeling of emptiness.

He must have slept, for when he came to he was tangled in her arms, and the heart that beat beneath his was slow and heavy. He raised his head just as her eyes fluttered open, all smokily green with satiation.

'Oh, Nico,' she sighed.

He traced the line of her lip with a lazy finger, and desire returned with a potent power that shook him. His mouth hardened. Keep it in perspective, he told himself.

'So, tell me all about this idea of yours,' he drawled.

Ella stared up at him, blinking her eyes in a long moment of confusion. 'Idea?' she questioned dazedly. What the hell was he talking about?

He shifted away from her fractionally. Distance gave perspective, and right now he needed it. She could weave an extraordinary kind of magic in his arms, but that was all. That was *all*.

He turned onto his side and propped himself up on his elbow, his eyes drifting over hers with a lazy look of amusement. 'You have forgotten your idea already, *cara*?' he teased. 'If it cannot last beyond the hour then it cannot be an idea of any substance!'

His words brought Ella crashing back to reality

with a painful jolt as she heard the mocking truth in them.

No substance.

No *substance*.

She had wanted to lie there murmuring sweet nothings, but he wanted to talk ideas! At least he had reminded her of her place in the scheme of things.

She composed her face and tried to rid it of the look of dreamy soppiness. Sweet heaven, Ella, you gave him your very soul itself just now, so make sure you claw back every last little bit of pride.

'Well.' She drew in a deep breath and the oxygen cleared her head. 'I will, of course, be making a full list of my proposed recommendations, but there is one thing which I think would have immediate impact— and that's to do something about the crowds around the Juan Lopez gallery. They're a real eyesore, and they make a very real congestion problem.'

Had he been expecting her to pout? To tell him prettily that she didn't want to talk about work at a time like this? Nico's eyes narrowed. The very unexpectedness of her remark and her cool thinking caught him on the back foot, so that—perversely—he found *himself* struggling to concentrate on her damned idea, and not on the pure, soft curves of her body.

He stared at her suspiciously. 'And what do you propose we do about that? Mardivino is rightly proud of her strong links with Lopez.'

'Move it,' she said simply.

His suspicious look intensified. 'Explain yourself.'

Oh, but now he sounded like an autocratic Royal! Yet, oddly enough, Ella's strength of mind and resolve was returning by the second. Was she going to suddenly become one of those wet-blanket kinds of women just because she had cried out in ecstasy in his arms? No, she was not! Whatever she was feeling inside, she would hide it, and he would not know because she would not let him.

Blocking the yearning desire to brush her fingertips over the dark curve of his jaw, she smiled. 'Solajoya is buzzing and thriving and it always will be—because it's a port *and* the capital. People travel here especially to see the works of Juan Lopez, so they don't *need* to be housed in Solajoya. So you move the gallery somewhere else. Somewhere the tourists don't bother to visit. Somewhere which could do with the extra revenue those tourists would bring. Somewhere like the village we just visited. Why not?'

There was a pause. 'Why not?' he echoed thoughtfully, and then the black eyes glittered. 'It sounds too simple.'

'The best ideas often are.' But so were the worst ones. Agreeing to a picnic with him had been simple, and making love simpler still. And yet no matter how much her calm, professional expression tried to hide it she was left with a deep, dark aching in her heart. Because it was never going to be more than this, and if she couldn't accept that she was going to get badly hurt. *Stick with what you know, Ella.*

'That village is badly in need of rejuvenating. Think what this could bring. A brand-new gallery, which would make the most of the paintings, and all the stuff which would go with it. Postcards, and prints, and a restaurant or two. Of course…' her ideas began to gallop away with her, 'You would have to be very careful not to destroy the character of the village, but I can't see you letting that happen.'

'Why, thank you, Gabriella,' he said mockingly.

She licked her lips, which were suddenly parched. 'So, will you think about it?'

'I will.'

'Good.' She had saved the day. She had done what she had set out to do, taken the heat out of the situation, but now she needed to get out of here and get her head together. She sat up and began to pull her dress down, but he reached out his hand to halt her.

'What are you doing?'

'What does it look like? I'm…' Her words dried in her mouth as his fingertips began to touch her bare breasts, skating enchanting little pathways across the already sensitised skin. She closed her eyes. 'I'm getting dressed.'

He felt the hot, hard jerk of desire as he pulled her against him, smoothing the palms of his hands over the silken globes of her buttocks and feeling her shudder. It was about time he showed her who was boss.

'Oh, no, you aren't,' he negated quietly.

She wanted to stop him.

No, she didn't.

She *tried* to stop him.

No, she didn't.

Trying to stop someone should amount to more than a distracted little shake of the head. If she had really been trying to stop him then she would not now be squirming with delight as he stroked and touched her, nor be touching him back and hearing him moan so softly.

Nor would her heart be leaping with a wild and delirious kind of joy as he entered her once more. Her last sane thought was that this perfect act was going to achieve the impossible. Leaving her feeling complete.

Yet achingly incomplete.

# CHAPTER TWELVE

THEY drove down the mountain road in silence, and for Ella it was a silence fraught with unanswered questions. There was none of the companionable ease she might have expected or hoped for after such a successful morning—which had culminated in that heartstoppingly erotic encounter.

For Nico had retreated.

She had seen it in his eyes once passion had faded. As if someone had suddenly changed the temperature of the tap while you were washing your hands, so that it had gone straight from warm to icy-cold, making you flinch. Even his features, which she had seen look so animated and alive during the act of love, were now simply cool and indifferent.

Oh, he had been sweet enough—he had buttoned up her dress and teased her, and drifted his lips over her skin in a teasing way—but it had felt as though he was simply going through the motions of how a lover *should* behave afterwards. There had been no sense of real closeness—no conviction that if she had asked him what was going on in that head of his he would have told her.

The intimacy that had been there both before and after they had made love had vanished. And something within her had been sapped. As if by pleasing her physically he had taken away her ability to talk to him as if he was just any man.

So, was this the end of her 'assignment'? Even if he did take up her suggestion about moving the gallery—did that entitle her to stay? Would she actually want to—was she just going to allow herself to be picked up and put down at will? A plaything for a prince...

She bit her lip and stared out of the window as the white rooftops of Solajoya began to appear.

Nico flicked her a glance.

Now what did he do?

He had a choice, of course. He could treat it as a one-off. Something he had badly wanted and that he had now been given, satisfying his hunger sufficiently enough to drive that hunger away. But it had not been. Even with that stiff, slightly defensive set of her shoulders, he found that he was still turned on. He still wanted to caress her, to run his fingertips over her until she opened up again, like a glorious flower—spreading her petals just for him, so that he could lose himself in their heady perfume.

He swore softly as he crashed a gear, and she turned her head, her eyebrows raised in question.

Nico glowered at the road ahead. He was a superb driver—good enough to grace the circuit of any international motor-race, dammit! So why was he acting like a nervous pupil out taking his test?

The car slid to a halt in front of L'Etoile, and, sucking in a deep breath to give her courage, Ella turned to him. She wasn't dealing with a normal man, she reminded herself, and she must not expect him to behave like one. No long lingering kiss, or promise to ring her. After all, they were in public now.

Keep it together, Ella, she told herself. Act like a sophisticated career-woman. If it was a one-off, then remember it as something very beautiful and take your heartache back to England with you, to nurse it in private.

She smiled. Take control. Give him a let-out. Give *yourself* a let-out. A plaything for a prince? *Never in a million years!* 'I guess I'd better think about booking my flight home.'

Her words took him by surprise. 'Home?' he demanded, his brow deepening into a frown.

'Of course.' The smile became easier—encouraged by the almost insulting look of astonishment on his face! Did his women usually cling with all the tenacity of a rock-climber hanging on for dear life? 'What is there to stay for now? I've made my recommendations to improve some of Mardivino's problems, and you've managed to have sex with me.'

'*Managed?*' he shot out, affronted. 'You make it sound as though you had nothing to do with it!'

'Do I?' Ella was enjoying herself now—how wonderful to see that look of indifference replaced by a genuine emotion, even if it *was* anger! 'Well, obviously that's not true. I—'

'How very good of you to concede that!' His

mocking words sliced right through hers, his eyes glittering at her in challenge.

'I was part of what happened.'

'Thank God for that,' he said drily.

'But there is no need for me to stay now. Not really.'

Nico's mouth hardened. She was right; there wasn't. The bottom line was that her job here *had* been a ruse. A threat. A demonstration of his power and privilege—and yet she had taken him at his word. He had presented her with a problem and she had coolly solved it. She had, in fact, exceeded all his expectations—both in and out of the bedroom. *But you haven't even taken her to the bedroom!* The voice in his head was taunting him, and his body began to ache even more as he realised just how much unfulfilled potential there was with Gabriella.

'I don't want you to go,' he said stubbornly.

She nearly said, *And Nico gets everything he wants.* Except that he didn't. No person did—not even princes—especially not princes. She thought of his lonely childhood, spent on show—brought out on high-days and holidays like a little mannequin. She had seen that for herself in all the photographs. Why on earth should she be surprised if he did not display 'normal' emotions?

She arched her eyebrows at him. 'Don't you?'

'No.'

She waited. She didn't want to go, either—but there was a difference between being honest enough to admit that and being a complete walk-over. Would he come even close to admitting that the feeling between them was powerful enough to make the obstacles of his birth seem momentarily insignificant? Or was that just her own interpretation?

He leaned towards her fractionally, so that she could breathe in the raw, feral scent of him, and his proximity weakened her, as he must have known it would. Say something that means something, she begged him silently. Tell me that even if you know it can't last, you care for me, even if it's just the tinest little bit.

'And surely you want to stay around to see your idea come to fruition?' he murmured.

She felt the sharp pain of a rejection he wasn't even aware of, but her face didn't give a flicker of reaction. It was time to start dealing with reality, not hopeless dreams. Unless she was prepared to do that she was onto a loser.

'I have a business to run back in England, Nico,' she reminded him gently. 'I can't stay around indefinitely.' But as soon as the words were out of her mouth she wished she could reach out and grab them back. Because it gave voice to a timespan. They asked for a time limit. She was asking the question she didn't have the guts to voice directly.

His eyes glittered, and he knew then that he must be up front with her. He wanted her—*Ah, si*—but on his terms—for there was no other way.

'I'd like you to stay on for a while, Ella. To put

your idea to Gianferro and to the planners, yes—but something more than that.' He shrugged, as if it didn't matter—*Dio*, it *didn't* matter! He would live if she said no. His eyes gleamed with dark intent. He had no intention of letting her say no. 'I want you as my lover, Gabriella,' he admitted softly. 'Just that.'

*Just that.*

As a declaration it was insulting.

Or just honest?

He was making up the rules, as he had probably done in relationships all his adult life, and Ella realised she could accept that—or not. It all came down to one thing…whether she was prepared to accept him unconditionally, or whether she was going to allow those unrealistic dreams to send her home.

He saw her silent tussle—the yearning in her eyes that she was doing her best to disguise—but he saw, too, the proud way she held her head, and suddenly it was the most irresistible of combinations.

'I want to kiss you,' he ground out, the blood heating like molten lava in his veins. He could feel the fire spreading over his skin. 'But I cannot do that. Not now and not here. Indeed, I cannot come to your suite here, for the same reason that you cannot visit me in my rooms at the palace—the gossips will learn of it and your life will be made hell.'

'And yours, too, of course, Nico,' she observed drily. 'Let's not forget that.'

'We must be discreet,' he said, as if she had not spoken.

Discreet. As Royal mistresses had been since the beginning of dynastic rule.

'I have a house just outside Solajoya,' he continued. 'We can use that whenever we please. It is very beautiful and very isolated.'

Just as he was. Ella stared at the ebony smoulder of his eyes, the soft curve of anticipation that made his lush lips so sensual. His strong, lean body was tensed and expectant. She could almost feel the pulsing of his desire as it shimmered through the air towards her, and it was a feeling that was met and matched by her own.

Shouldn't she just take away what she had experienced in his arms? Take it away to remember it with pleasure? Like a golden treasure to be pulled out on rainy days, to remind her of a time that had been both precious and matchless? There could be no future in a relationship with this man; the only outcome that lay ahead was certain heartbreak. And not, she suspected, simply because of his Royal position.

She remembered the way he had switched from warm and giving to cool and indifferent after they had made love. Surely an ability to compartmentalise like that was a much bigger obstacle than his lofty status? Was she hoping that he would change? That everything would change and that they would walk off towards the sunset, hand in hand?

Deep in her heart, she knew what she *should* do.

So what was stopping her?

He was. Just him. Just by being Nico. The very

essence of the man himself. She had wanted him from the first moment she had set eyes on him, and the wanting had only increased. She had wanted him when she had thought he had nothing, and she wanted him still.

'I don't know,' she said truthfully, but the doubt in her voice sounded like an invitation to be convinced.

'We could go there later, *cara mia*.' The velvet voice brushed deliberately over her senses. 'Spend the night in each other's arms. One night. Tonight. Why would you say no to that?'

With a mixture of excitement and dread, Ella knew that she could not resist. One night—what harm could it do? She nodded slowly, as if she was giving the matter consideration, but in reality it was to prevent him from seeing the vulnerability in her eyes, which was making her feel as raw and as naïve as a teenager.

She lifted her head, and now her gaze was proud and fearless. She had made her decision and she was going to enjoy every minute of it.

'Why not?' she said lightly, and pushed open the car door. 'Will you pick me up? Or shall I put on a dark cloak and wait on a shadowed corner?'

He laughed, suddenly filled with a reckless excitement. 'I will pick you up at eight,' he said. 'And I will cook for you again.'

But food was the last thing on Ella's mind as she soaked away the picnic dust from her body in a long bath.

No doubts, she told herself sternly as she brushed her damp hair. That's not the point of the exercise.

And the point of the exercise was...?

She slammed her hairbrush down on the dresser. Pleasure. Enjoyment. Simple, normal stuff—and she was *not* going to get heavy.

She slipped out of the side-door of L'Etoile to find his car waiting, and she slid into the seat beside him.

He smiled as he turned the ignition key. 'You smell like flowers, *cara*. A meadow of flowers.'

She was glad that the dim light concealed her blush of pleasure. But it's just the continental way, she reminded herself as the powerful car purred its way out of the capital. The men were schooled in elegant compliments in a way that Englishmen simply were not. She had found that out at the very beginning.

But sweet words could turn a woman's head, even if that was the last thing in the world she needed, and Ella felt an unbearable sense of expectation as he negotiated the bends. In a way, this tryst was nothing but a cold—or hot!—blooded sensual arrangement between two consenting adults, and yet not even that knowledge could still her mounting excitement. Soon she would be in his arms again, and suddenly that was the only thing that mattered.

The house was in darkness as he unlocked it, but he clicked a switch and light immediately flooded from a huge chandelier. Yet Ella barely noticed the grand and elegant proportions, the pieces of antique

French furniture that were dotted around the hallway, for he pulled her into his arms with a hungry groan, burying his face in her hair and breathing deeply, like a man who had been underwater for a long time.

He moved away and cupped her face between his palms, his black eyes glittering with an intensity that was brighter than the light overhead.

'Bed,' he whispered, and, taking her hand in his, led her up a wide and curving staircase.

Her mouth was too dry for words—but what use were words at a time like this? She was long past the stage of pretty protests that maybe they should eat supper first, or perhaps they should have a drink, because she wanted neither.

This felt grown-up—almost too grown-up—yet nothing could stop the heated longing that was clamouring its way through her veins, the longing to feel his skin next to her once again. Nico as Nico—stripped of everything—just a man of flesh against her flesh.

He pushed open a door to reveal a beautiful bed, hung with richly lavish embroidered drapes, and he turned her towards him, his eyes holding hers for one long, impenetrable second.

'Now kiss me,' he instructed quietly. 'Kiss me, *cara mia*.'

It was a command that she could not have resisted even if the building had been tumbling down around them. She looped her arms around his neck, stood up on tiptoe and pressed her mouth to his, and his soft moan filled her with delight and with daring.

As his lips opened beneath hers, and their tongues laced in languid exploration, she pressed her body closer to his and felt his breath mingling with hers as he gave another moan.

It was as if they had each been schooled in what was to come next for they moved in synchrony, in a silent wordless dance towards the bed, as if they had practised the steps over and over again, and yet Ella knew she had never moved like that before. Had he?

With hungry, conspiratorial smiles, they slid onto the bed.

'Gabriella—'

But she touched her finger to his lips to silence him and began to unbutton his shirt. Words would destroy the fantasy that he was hers—at least with her body she could pretend.

She had never taken the lead quite like this before, and there was a vague corner of her mind that wondered whether such a dominant man would allow her to. But her disquiet was only fleeting, for she could see from the look of rapture on his face that he was loving it.

She trickled her fingertips down over the tiny hard nipples, tracing butterfly circles around the sensitised flesh, and his hard, lean body writhed with pleasure.

'*Che cosa state facendo a me?*' he groaned softly.

Her hands moved to the hard, flat planes of his hips. 'In English, please!' she teased.

But he shook his head, the words forgotten and already redundant.

She undressed him as slowly as she could, until the tension between them was so fraught that it was almost unbearable. Her hands were shaking as she skated the silken camiknickers down over her hips, and then she climbed on top of him. Their eyes met in a silence broken only by their rapid breathing as she slowly lowered herself onto him, encasing him in her tight, exquisite heat.

And that was when it became too much. A little cry escaped from her lips, and suddenly she was trembling and out of control.

He was watching her, and he understood perfectly, pulling her face down to his to kiss her and tangling his hand in the satin hair before turning her onto her side and beginning to move inside her.

Ella gasped, and it was much more than the feeling of him filling her, deep and hard and true——it was the way that their gazes were locked, watching each other's reaction in a way that was almost scarily intimate.

She thrilled to see the pleasure that rippled up from his body to make his face relax in helpless rapture, and his delight fed hers until she could watch him no more. Until the waves that had been building and building rocked over her with a power that obliterated everything except the shuddering man within her arms.

He watched her orgasm, holding back his own, almost resenting it, because he didn't want this to stop. The urge to give in was unbearably strong now. *Signore dolce*, but he was having to battle with his body not to go under with each deep thrust. It was that feeling all over again. Like reaching the top of the mountain. Or falling from the stars.

He began to cry out then, his release bittersweet as he was caught up in spasms of pleasure so sharp that he felt he might die right at that moment. And then he let go, while the warm waves drifted over him, his eyes closing as he breathed in the soft, feminine fragrance of her.

For a while he held her tightly, but then suddenly and abruptly he rolled away and lay staring up at the ceiling, where the moon was making flickering silent movies in monochrome.

And Ella felt the sensation of loneliness creep in, where there had been only pleasure and fulfillment. He had done it again, she realised. Shut down. Shut her out. The closeness, the sense of complete unity— that was purely physical. Maybe he didn't realise he was doing it…

'Hey,' she whispered. 'Don't do that!'

She reached her hand out to him and ran her fingertip from shoulder to elbow. He turned his head to look at her, but he was not smiling.

'Don't do what?' he questioned coldly.

The tone of his voice should have warned her, but Ella was in such a state of helpless rapture that she chose not to heed it. She shrugged. How could he learn if she didn't teach him? 'You go all distant after we've made love. It can still be intimate, you know,' she added softly. 'Once it's over.'

Her flame-red hair looked like quietly gleaming fire in the light of the moon, but her eyes were in shadow and he knew that he could not continue to take from her—not when she gave so generously. For that had not been just mind-blowing sex—that had been making love. That was why it had felt so different. So wild. So free. So dangerous.

Nico knew what she was offering, and that if he continued to accept it without any return—or even with the unspoken promise of some return—then he would be nothing more than an emotional thief. However much it might hurt, he had to tell her. Though wasn't there a part of him that hoped that she might forgive him anything in the face of honesty?

His eyes were bleak as they searched her face. 'I don't love you, Gabriella,' he said quietly.

## CHAPTER THIRTEEN

ELLA let Nico's words sink in, like a heavy rock disappearing without trace into the murky water, but her initial feeling was one of an almost euphoric relief. It was like going to the doctor and demanding to know the truth about a prognosis, because only then would you be able to tackle the problem head-on.

And cure it.

But the euphoria was almost immediately replaced by a feeling of real fear, and she wanted to say to him, *I know! I'm not stupid, Nico! I've known all along, and I would have been able to come to terms with it in my own time and in my own way if only you could have pretended.*

*Just for one night.*

*One beautiful make-believe night.*

Cure it?

How the hell was she going to do that? By playing dumb? By feigning ignorance? By saying in a cool, collected way, *What the hell are you talking about?*

No. He had had a lifetime of people telling him what they did not mean. Skating over the surface. Hours of conversation that was not real conversation, merely superficial small talk. If she was going to take anything away from her brief fling with him, it was going to be honesty.

And pride.

'I know that, Nico,' she said, and her voice was almost gentle. Funny, that. How softness should appear from nowhere, utterly concealing the shattering knowledge that this would be the last time. But it wasn't his fault. Not really. He was the man he was, not the one she wanted him to be.

He frowned, as if this was not the reaction he had been expecting. 'I'm twenty-eight,' he grated. 'And I don't want to settle down. With anyone. I don't *need* to settle down. And when I do it's going to be with someone—'

'Someone suitable,' she cut in wryly, seeing his narrow-eyed look of irritation. But hell, hadn't he interrupted *her* enough times in the past? 'I know that, too, Nico. Why the hell are you bothering to tell me all this?'

And why now? Couldn't he have waited until the morning and left her with the memory beautiful and intact? Not tarnished with the bitterness of truth.

She sat up, the turmoil of her thoughts almost making her forget that she was naked until she saw the smoky response of his eyes. He reached for her, as if conditioned to do so, but she shook him off. 'Don't,' she said steadily. 'Please don't touch me.'

There had never been a situation in his life that he could not charm his way out of, but he could see that she meant it. Stubborn, obstinate woman. He stifled a sigh. 'Come on, let's go and eat something.'

But Gabriella shook her head. How easy it would be to gloss over it. To go downstairs to his kitchen and let him seduce her with his cooking and conversation, to sip wine and become lulled, so that eventually the stark reality would fade into the background. And then they would kiss again and make love—only it would not be the same—how could it be? Because, despite the odds being stacked against them having any kind of future together, that hadn't prevented a stupid side of her hoping that maybe they could.

But his words had destroyed all hope, and without hope what was left?

Pride, she reminded herself. She still had that.

'No,' she said, shaking her head, trying to keep the sadness from her voice. 'There is no point. I want to go back to L'Etoile right now, and tomorrow morning I'm catching a flight back to England.'

He swore softly. 'Damn you, Gabriella,' he responded, and his words were equally quiet, but tinged with acid. 'I've been honest with you,' he said bitterly, wishing that he had said nothing until the morning. 'Why can't you just accept that?'

'Accept your terms without question, you mean?' she asked stiffly. 'Terms which don't give a stuff about my feelings? Sorry, Nico, but you can't have it all ways. You can't play the poor little misunderstood Prince who needs to keep his identity secret because of all the baggage that goes with his title and then turn round and arrogantly demand the unquestioning obedience which is part and parcel of that title!'

'How dare you say that to me?' he demanded.

'How dare I?' Her green eyes flashed fire at him. 'I'll tell you how I dare! Doesn't the fact that we've just made love give me any rights at all? Or do you treat all your women as though they are commodities? To be used until they begin to threaten you, or make demands on you which aren't part of your Royal game plan?'

'That is enough!' he rapped out.

'No, it is not enough!' she retorted. 'Maybe it's time someone started responding to you as a normal human being—but you can't take it when they do, can you? You profess to hate the restriction of Royal life, but you can't wait to hide behind it when it suits you!'

'Hide?' he echoed furiously. 'Me? *Hide?*'

Ella gave a cynical laugh as she realised she really *had* struck home. 'So I've offended your macho image, have I, Nico?' she questioned, and her eyes were sparking a challenge at him. 'Don't you know there's more to being a real man than jumping on motorbikes and endangering your life into the bargain?'

'Enough!' he snapped.

But she was driven on by a need so relentless that she could not have stopped even if she had wanted to.

'You say that you have a problem with Gianferro?

Well, I'm not surprised—he's worried sick about you! Just how long do you intend to carry on being ''The Daredevil Prince'', with your crazy stunts? Until you're an old man of fifty—tearing up the mountain roads on a motorbike? How sad it that?'

'I am not listening to another word of this!' he raged. 'I'll wait for you downstairs!'

'Yes—run away, why don't you? You'll probably spend the rest of your life running away from the truth!'

For a moment there was an incredulous silence. 'Running away?' he echoed.

'I think so. Subconsciously.' She stared at him, poised on this moment of revelation like a diver about to plunge into the water, and she dived in fearlessly. 'But you'll never be happy until you work out what it is you're running *from*.' She stared at him, waiting breathlessly for his response, like a condemned woman praying for leniency from the judge. But he simply gave a bitter and sarcastic laugh as he reached for his shirt.

'You'd better get dressed,' he said, barely flicking her a glance.

In a way it was the worst possible reaction. At least when he had been furious she had felt they were still connected in some way—as if a row was validation that there had been more between them than simply sex. But this new, barely feigned boredom was humiliating. As if he couldn't wait to be rid of her.

Had her words wounded him? She had spoken in

anger, yes—but she had felt justified in doing so. Her intention had been to enlighten and help him, not to hurt him.

Tentatively she reached towards the ruffled dark hair, but he moved away and slid his legs over the bed. He pulled on his jeans with a dismissive gesture that broke her heart into tiny pieces and she realised she had blown it for ever—detonated it with her harsh words.

No. He had blown it, too—by enforcing rigid rules that put paid to any growing closeness between them.

She reached for her crumpled camiknickers and shook them, seeing him watching her, the way the movement made her unfettered breasts swing freely. She saw his mouth tighten.

'Hurry up,' he snapped, and walked out and left her, his face an icy mask of haughty *froideur*.

With trembling hands she dressed in that moonlit room, her skin still flushed and rosy with the aftermath of their incredible lovemaking. And as she straightened up from fastening her sandals she caught a glimpse of herself in the Venetian mirror that hung over the ornate fireplace.

There she was, in her chainstore dress, her hair all mussed. The strange half-light cast by the moon only added to the surreal image in the mirror. She had no place here, nor ever would.

Slowly she began to descend the wide, curving staircase. Nico waited at the bottom, his dark, glittering eyes watching her as if she was some new species he had encountered and he was unsure of just what she was going to do next.

And she watched him, with eyes that were equally uncertain.

Wasn't there a part of her that regretted her words? A part of her that would now be responsive to having her mind changed? If Nico took her into his arms and kissed her and tried to cajole her into staying, would she honestly be able to resist him?

With an effort he tore his eyes away from the silken thrust of her thighs as she came down the stairs towards him.

'Let's go,' he said shortly, and gave an insulting glance at his watch. 'You might not be hungry, *cara*, but I am. I'll drop you off at the hotel and then I'm going out to dinner.'

Who with? she wondered. But the painful lurch of her heart was caused not by vague imagined jealousies, but by the realisation that already she was swiftly moving into Nico's past.

Soon she would be little more than a hazy memory.

## CHAPTER FOURTEEN

THE trouble was that there was no one Ella could tell—not really—because even to herself it sounded completely unbelievable. What would her parents say—or Rachel, or her best friend Celia—if she suddenly blurted out the reason for her sudden mood swings and the tears in her eyes that swam up without warning?

*Well, it's like this. I've fallen in love with a prince, but he doesn't love me. We've had an affair and now it's over, and I have to move on and get on with my normal life.*

In the end she had to come up with some explanation, so she came up with one that said it all.

*It's a man.*

Then they all understood, and there was no need for any more explanation at all. No one particularly cared where he was or who he was—although Celia had a pretty good try—because the bottom line was that he was out of the picture and Ella was left nursing a broken heart.

And when she stopped to think about it that really was the fundamental issue. It didn't matter that Nico was a prince. If he had been a banker or a restaurant owner or a truck driver would her pain have been any less?

Of course not. Love hurt. It sliced through your heart with its particular and specific pain and you just had to wait for time to heal it. That boring prediction that everyone made. Time heals. On an intellectual level you knew it was true, but on an emotional one— well, you just couldn't imagine not living in this state of misery for the rest of your life.

Her departure from Mardivino had been hurried and inglorious. Oh, an elegant car had arrived to take her to the airport, but it had been driven by a chauffeur, not by Nico.

Her only contact with him after that night, when he had driven her home in a simmering silence, had been a terse and factual telephone call when he had informed her of flight times.

The only unexpected touch had come at the end of the conversation, when Nico had added, or perhaps *growled* might be a more accurate description of his tone, 'Gianferro thinks that your idea is an inspired one.'

And because she had been hanging onto her composure only by a thread, her response had come out as cool and sardonic. 'Please tell him that I am delighted to have been of service.'

So there you had it, thought Ella as she stared out of the window into her garden. Even the weather was reflecting her mood. It was one of those grey, depressing days when the clouds seemed so low they could touch your head, spilling out relentless sheets of rain.

It had been raining ever since she'd arrived home, and now the lawn was like a quagmire, with great boggy puddles splashed by the falling stair-rods.

Even by mid-morning the day did not seem to have lifted at all, and Ella had to light a lamp. She switched the radio on to find that a faded television personality was enjoying a renewed lease of fame by trekking to remote places all over the globe.

Maybe I should do something like that? Ella thought. Change of scenery.

She found that she missed Mardivino—but who wouldn't? She couldn't think of a single person who would not have ached for those clear blue skies and sapphire waters, and the green-clothed mountains and white-capped houses of the capital.

She fiddled with the radio, swapping the explorer for the more soothing sounds of classical music, and had just made herself a large pot of coffee when there was a ring at the doorbell. She sighed.

Please don't be Rachel, she thought. Or Celia. Or any other well-meaning friend who had decided that she needed 'taking out of herself'. For a second she thought about not answering it, but only for a second.

No.

The world wasn't going to go away, and nor should it.

When she pulled the door open, it was with a smile. Funny, that. Inside, your heart could be breaking into a thousand little pieces, but somehow you managed to disguise it with a bright smile.

But the smile froze into a burning slash on her lips, for it was not Rachel, or Celia, but Nico who stood there, with raindrops sparkling on his black hair, his face shadowed and his big, strong body so alive and virile.

He looked…

Ella swallowed.

He looked both man and prince. Despite the soaking flying jacket and the faded jeans, there was something indefinably regal about his proud and autocratic bearing.

Never had he looked more desirable, nor quite so unobtainable.

He stared down at her upturned face, pale and heart-shaped, with eyes like two enormous emeralds, and saw there the swift look of pain and regret. For a moment he almost turned away. Perhaps the feelings they aroused in each other were too intense—too incompatible with life itself—especially *his* life. Perhaps she had come to that conclusion herself. But he knew that he had to find out.

'*Ciao, bella,*' he said softly, and then, even more softly, 'Gabriella.'

He was the only person who had ever called her that. As if by using her true name he had awoken the true woman who had always lain beneath the surface. A woman who could love and live and feel and hurt—

a woman with the same passions as him, only he sublimated those passions using damned *machines*!

Ella stared at him, wanting to pinch herself, trying to get used to the fact that he was not a figment of her imagination but standing here, on her doorstep.

She thought that he looked different. Harder, and leaner. Edgy. His jaw was dark-shadowed—taunting her with its potent symbol of virility. Seeing him again made the grey day suddenly seem bright, and Ella felt her heart melt. Oh, God—would she ever be able to look at him without curling up inside for love of him?

'Nico!' she exclaimed. 'What are you doing here?'

'Getting wet,' he said wryly.

'Oh, God—you'd better come in!'

His lips were curved in a rueful smile. When in his life had he ever been left standing in the pouring rain on someone's doorstep?

'Give me your jacket,' she said hurriedly, because it was easier to compose herself when she was doing something, and he *was* very wet. But her hands were shaking as she hung the dripping jacket up. *Compose herself?* Who did she think she was kidding?

She ran her eyes over his face, not daring to nurture the tiny flicker of hope she felt. Just because he was here, it didn't mean anything. 'Why are you here?' she whispered.

His very presence here was a statement that normally would have been enough. But it was not enough. She had accused him of many things, but the one that had struck home had been *running away*. And using circumstances and privilege and things— yes, things—as a substitute for reality. Stark reality. Which was sometimes painful but which you could not hide from for ever if you wanted to live in any degree of peace.

But Nico was a man who had never explained his feelings before—never had to—and, as with learning all new skills, he found himself in the long-forgotten position of being a novice.

'I've got rid of my bike,' he said.

Ella blinked as her foolish little fantasies crumbled into dust. Whatever she might have been secretly hoping for, it had not been to talk about his damned motorbike! Her face was expressionless. 'Have you?' she questioned woodenly.

He realised that this was not what she wanted to hear. Like a child learning to swim, he attempted a second, tentative stroke. 'I don't want to be a "sad old man of fifty careering around the hills."'

He was throwing her words back at her. Ella bit her lip. 'I shouldn't have said that—'

'On the contrary, *cara mia*—you said exactly the right thing.'

'I did?'

He heard the disbelief in her voice and knew it was justified. 'How else could I learn?' he questioned simply, and he smiled as he saw her lips part in sheer astonishment. 'I didn't want to hear it at the time, but then no one had ever spoken quite like that to me before. I don't want those thrills and spills any more. They mean nothing. They count for nothing because they are not real.' Now his black gaze was very steady. 'But you thrill me, Ella, and you are real. Very real.'

She could scarcely breathe, but she knew that she wanted more than she suspected he was offering. And more than that she needed him to say it again, as if only repetition could convince her that he meant it, that it wasn't just a whim because the physical thing between them was such dynamite.

'You'll get good sex with another woman, Nico, you know you will.'

His face darkened. Stubborn, obtuse woman! 'I'm not talking about sex!'

'You're not?'

In the background he could hear the rippling notes of a piano being played, and the music drifted the most poignant sensation of contentment over his skin. 'No.'

'Then...what are you talking about?'

Nico scowled. 'I don't know. It feels like love.' This was an unimaginable admission, but it was not quite the truth. Hadn't she peeled back all the layers of his life, forcing him to look deep into the true and sometimes painful core of it? Did he now dare? For a man who had spent his life taking risks, there had never been one that seemed quite as daunting as this one. He shrugged his shoulders like a little boy. 'It is love,' he admitted. 'I am in love with you. I love you, Gabriella.'

'Oh, God,' she breathed. 'Oh, Nico.'

Her eyes were dazzling him—blinding him with a fervent emerald gaze that was more vivid than the shades found in any ocean. And in them he saw what she felt for him, a wordless declaration of how much he meant to her.

But was it enough? Would she be prepared to relinquish her freedom for a Royal life, aspects of which she professed to despise?

'Do you think we can have a future together?' he questioned softly.

Ella shook her head. 'I can't think beyond the next second,' she declared, her voice breaking. 'And if you don't come here and hold me then I think I might just die.'

Taking her in his arms was the easiest thing he had ever had to do, and to feel her arms wrapping tightly around his neck as though she was never going to let him go felt like coming home. Nico closed his eyes against the scented silk of her hair.

It defied all logic and sense, this feeling—more precious and more rare than any of the priceless jewels contained in his family's palaces. And he had only ever experienced it with her. Only her. In her arms. Like this. For this feeling men relinquished kingdoms, and he could understand exactly why.

'Shh,' he soothed as he felt her begin to tremble against him. 'I know. Believe me, *cara mia*, I know.'

He tipped her chin up and their eyes sizzled frantic seeking messages, questions answered without a single word being spoken. And then his mouth moved to blot out all the pain and the heartache, touching down on her lips with a tenderness she had never thought he would show, and she cupped his face in her hands and tenderly kissed him back.

And when eventually they drew back from it their eyes were dazed.

'*Cielo dolce,*' murmured Nico, shaken by the power and beauty of the embrace, for he had never known that a kiss could be anything other than foreplay. How little he knew! How much to learn. He stroked her face, like a blind man seeking to see by touch alone.

Ella stared up at him. Could this really be happening? And even if it was, what happened now? When two people were in love, of course they talked about a future—but this was not as it was for other people. How could it be? She pressed her finger to his cheek, which was still cool and faintly damp. 'We can't talk here. You're frozen—come and let's sit by the fire.'

The sweet, sane normality of her words made him smile. 'You've lit a fire? But it's only September.'

'And freezing! Come through. I'm going to pour us a brandy.'

He held his hands out to the blaze and sank down. It pleased her to see him sprawling on her rug, his long legs stretched out in front of him. She sploshed a measure of brandy into two glasses and went and sat down beside him. Only when they had sipped and put the drinks down in the hearth did she turn to him.

'So what has changed you from the icy man who stormed away to this...' She traced his lips with her finger, as if to confirm that he was real and not some dream that would evaporate in a second.

He opened his mouth and trapped the finger, sucking on it until it was quite wet. Seeing her eyes darken, he took it out again and absently wrapped it in a fold of his cashmere sweater, and left it there.

'You did. You changed me,' he said softly. 'You forced me to look at things I did not wish to. You made me see that, yes, I *was* running away—all the time—running from feelings, because feelings can hurt.' He shrugged. 'But, more than that, you made me see my life for what it was, and without you it is empty. I want to be with you, Gabriella.'

She forced herself to be practical, because if she started slipping into her greatest wish and then circumstances snatched it away again... 'But Gianferro will never allow it!'

'Because?'

'Because I'm a commoner and you're a prince! He will never approve of me!'

'He certainly *does* approve of you,' he contradicted drily. 'He was storming round the throne room yesterday morning, asking what it was that you had which could make me see sense, when he had been trying to drum it into me for years!'

'Approval is one thing,' she said slowly, 'but us

having a life together is quite something else. And how can we? I live here and you live in Mardivino. You can't live here, for practical reasons, and if I came out to join you in Mardivino then we'd have to conduct our affair in secret.'

'Not if we were married.'

Ella stared at him. 'I'm sorry?'

'Sudden onset of defective hearing, Gabriella?' he teased.

'Did you just mention marriage?'

'I did.'

'You want to marry me?'

'Of course I do! Don't you want to marry me?' He shot her a look of affectionate reprimand. 'Though you still have not told me you love me!'

'Of...' She drew a deep breath. 'Oh, my God—of course I love you, my darling, darling Nico—you know that I do.'

'*Si,*' he agreed, with arrogant contentment. 'I do.'

'But we can't get *married*!'

'Why not?'

'It's too soon!'

He shook his dark head and placed his hand on his heart in the most romantic gesture that Ella could ever have imagined. 'No, it isn't,' he contradicted softly. 'In fact, in this we are following tradition, for Royal courtships are never long drawn out.'

'But won't you need Gianferro's permission?'

'I would marry you without it, *cara mia.*' His eyes

glittered. 'But my resistance is academic, since he has already given it.'

Ella blinked. 'S-seriously?'

He nodded. *'Oui, c'est vrai.'*

She narrowed her eyes suspiciously. 'You told me that *Italian* was the language of love!'

He smiled. 'And so it is,' he agreed softly. 'But French is the language of the law—and marriage is both—a combination of love and obligation.' There was a pause, a silence broken only by the loud drumming of a heart. Was that his, or hers? 'Will you marry me, Gabriella?'

She didn't blurt her answer out. She gave it the consideration that she knew she must, for a Royal marriage *was* different. She loved him, yes, but obligation and duty were paramount if they were to be happy together, and she must only accept his offer if she could be certain that she would make him a good wife.

'Oh, yes, Nico,' she said softly, fervently. 'I would be proud and honoured to be your wife.'

## EPILOGUE

EVERYONE loved a Royal wedding, and Mardivino was no exception. The world's press went crazy about the story of the youngest of the three darkly handsome princes falling in love with an 'ordinary' girl from England.

It was all a bit overwhelming.

In the end, Ella decided to confound all the pundits who were wildly predicting which of the world's most exclusive designers would be lucky enough to create her wedding gown. She opted instead for a beautifully simple dress of finest white lawn, lovingly crafted by her mother's dressmaker. In her arms she carried a bouquet of that most English of flowers—pure white roses.

'Understated is the new black!' screamed the pundits.

But for Ella it did not matter that they were marrying in Solajoya's exquisite medieval cathedral, with world leaders and Royalty among the congregation. She was marrying the man she loved, who loved her, and that was the only thing that counted.

When she looked into his eyes at the altar everything else retreated, for all she could see was Nico, and only Nico—her love and her life.

Nico had given her a free hand to refurnish his house outside the city, but they had also been given a suite of rooms in the palace itself. It could all have been a bit daunting, but Ella's love outshone everything else, and she took on her new role with both zeal and pleasure.

They would work together, too.

Although they would not live together until after the marriage, Nico had introduced her to all areas of his life, and she had discovered just how many different schemes he was involved with. Little wonder he hadn't had time to visit every single village on the island—but part of his new regeneration programme was to explore the under-funded towns, with Ella by his side.

He had ordered the relocation of Solajoya's main museum, and he wanted her to help plan a worldwide tour of Juan Lopez's work—to bring the 'artist's artist' to a much wider arena.

The new gallery was to be opened in the village by the new Princess before a wildly enthusiastic local population, grateful that a share of the island's tourism was now putting them firmly on the map. Architects and town planners had been flown in to oversee the gentle expansion, which was designed to blend into the scenery, not bleed it of all its natural simplicity.

Gianferro had asked for an audience with her soon after their engagement had been announced and she had flown out to the island to prepare for the wedding.

Her stomach had been churning as she had walked along the gilded corridor towards his suite of offices. He had given them his approval, yes, but what if secretly he had doubts about her ability to make a good wife and princess?

But Ella needn't have had any fears. His hard face had softened on seeing the look of anxiety in hers, and he had patted a space on the brocade sofa beside him.

'Come, Gabriella,' he had murmured. 'And tell me what magic you have worked on Nico.'

'No magic,' she had responded shyly. 'Just love.'

The black eyes, so like his brother's, had gleamed. 'I had intended to ask whether you really do love him,' he said. 'But I can see now that the question is superfluous—for it shines like the sun at noon from your eyes.'

'Ooh, Gianferro is *my* kind of man,' Celia had whispered adoringly on the morning of the ceremony, as she'd tugged at the pale pink lawn of her bridesmaid dress. 'Any chance you could do a bit of matchmaking?'

But Ella had shaken her head. 'I don't think so. He's a loner,' she'd said. Gianferro would soon be King, for their father's health was ailing fast—and to be King was a lonely destiny. Princes abounded, but Kings were few. Nico had been able to dispense with a certain amount of expectation by marrying her, a commoner, simply because he was the youngest son—with a lessened burden of responsibility riding on his shoulders.

But Gianferro's destiny was mapped out. When he took a bride she would *have* to be suitable. And when Ella looked at his sensual yet restless face, she wondered just how he would cope with the reality of having to marry a virgin bride.

Prince Guido had flown in at the very last moment, and Ella had witnessed an extraordinary phenomenon, as every female in his vicinity had taken on a look of longing that bordered on the incandescent. He was a remarkably good-looking man, she acknowledged, but his black eyes were bored, almost jaded.

'So you have beaten me to the altar, Nico,' he had drawled at the pre-nuptial ball.

'No surprise there!' his brother had responded drily. 'You have a wish to be married, Guido?' he'd added curiously.

'No wish at all,' had come the mocking response. 'I'm happy as I am.'

'Are you?' Ella had asked suddenly, and both brothers had turned to her. Nico had not mirrored Guido's surprise—but then he was growing used to her candid way of saying what she really thought!

Guido's eyes had narrowed. 'Of course,' he'd said lightly. 'I enjoy my life of self-imposed exile, for there is none of the expectation which surrounds me here. No damned matrons clucking and introducing me to their darling daughters.' And he'd given a rather bitter laugh as one of the said matrons had begun bearing down on him, her diamonds almost blinding them, a look of grim determination on her face. 'Forgive me,' he'd murmured. 'But it's time I wasn't here.'

'I'm afraid that Guido is a bit of a cynic where women are concerned,' Nico had confided to her later. Their guests had gone and they were standing side by side on the terrace, gazing up at the stars and a crescent moon.

She had turned to him with an expression of mock surprise. 'Never!'

Nico had laughed.

They did a lot of laughing. They held each other tight at night and thanked God they had found one another.

Ella had left an old life behind, but so had Nico, and the one they had found together was better than their wildest dreams.

**If you enjoyed what you just read,
then we've got an offer you can't resist!**

# Take 2 bestselling
# love stories FREE!
# Plus get a FREE surprise gift!

**Clip this page and mail it to Harlequin Reader Service®**

| IN U.S.A. | IN CANADA |
|---|---|
| 3010 Walden Ave. | P.O. Box 609 |
| P.O. Box 1867 | Fort Erie, Ontario |
| Buffalo, N.Y. 14240-1867 | L2A 5X3 |

**YES!** Please send me 2 free Harlequin Presents® novels and my free surprise gift. After receiving them, if I don't wish to receive anymore, I can return the shipping statement marked cancel. If I don't cancel, I will receive 6 brand-new novels every month, before they're available in stores! In the U.S.A., bill me at the bargain price of $3.80 plus 25¢ shipping & handling per book and applicable sales tax, if any*. In Canada, bill me at the bargain price of $4.47 plus 25¢ shipping & handling per book and applicable taxes**. That's the complete price and a savings of at least 10% off the cover prices—what a great deal! I understand that accepting the 2 free books and gift places me under no obligation ever to buy any books. I can always return a shipment and cancel at any time. Even if I never buy another book from Harlequin, the 2 free books and gift are mine to keep forever.

106 HDN DZ7Y
306 HDN DZ7Z

| Name | (PLEASE PRINT) | |
|---|---|---|
| Address | Apt.# | |
| City | State/Prov. | Zip/Postal Code |

*Not valid to current Harlequin Presents® subscribers.*

*Want to try two free books from another series?*
*Call 1-800-873-8635 or visit www.morefreebooks.com.*

\* Terms and prices subject to change without notice. Sales tax applicable in N.Y.
\*\* Canadian residents will be charged applicable provincial taxes and GST.
   All orders subject to approval. Offer limited to one per household.
   ® are registered trademarks owned and used by the trademark owner and or its licensee.

PRES04R                              ©2004 Harlequin Enterprises Limited